# DARK ANGELS OF ZEUS

# Gary W. Babb

# DARK ANGELS OF ZEUS

DOUBLE DRAGON

ISBN  978-1-78695-478-7

Double Dragon
is an imprint of
Fiction4All

Published 2020
*Fiction4All*
*www.fiction4all.com*

Cover Art by Deron Douglas
www.derondouglas.ca

# Chapter 1
## In the Beginning

"Zeus!" After a long pause without a response Apollo yelled, "ZEUS!"

"YES, Yes, what do you want?" Zeus snapped. He had been preoccupied with the vision in the viewing mist on the dais below encircled by the assembly of Olympian gods. Four obvious Omega possessed mortals pursued a fifth mortal radiating an Alpha golden aura. The angry red, demon auras of the Omega mortals were strong and radiant, while the golden Alpha aura shown dim and weak, yet visible enough to identify him as an Alpha descendant spirit.

Apollo, apologetic but insistent, said, "Father, we must contact the Titan Assembly before all the remaining Alphas are destroyed."

As if to accent Apollo's statement, the four Omega mortals caught the fifth mortal and began mutilating and dismembering him with their shimmering swords. The fifth mortal never had a chance and hadn't even offered up a defense. The Alpha spirit obviously wasn't awake within him, and he wouldn't have an inkling of an idea what was happening to him or why. He would not be able to see the Omega auras nor access any of his ancient dormant powers. The poor man was terrified and died horribly along with his inactive Alpha spirit. The golden Alpha aura in the likeness of a hawk was the last to die as it floundered and flapped it wings ever more slowly until it melted into the ground and disappeared completely.

5

Zeus said, "I know! Dammit, I know, but I haven't spoken to the Titan Assembly since they exiled us to this world those thousands of years ago."

Hera screeched, "Well, it's your own cursed fault! The immortal Titan women were never enough for you, and you and the other immortals just had to fornicate with all those mortal women. That interracial mixing caused the separation of Alpha and Omega."

"SILENCE, WIFE!" Zeus bellowed, stabbing a warning finger in the air toward her, bristling with energy and barely controlled lighting. His deep, resonating voice and warning reverberated throughout the chamber, causing many of the gods, including Hera, to recoil in fear and silence. "Now is not the time to rehash the past. We have more important things to worry about."

Poseidon leaned forward on his throne toward Zeus and said, "True enough, brother, but I have to agree with Apollo. We must act quickly or we are doomed. At the rate Omega is seeking out and destroying Alpha we will not have any Alphas remaining to fight the coming war. We are already vastly outnumbered. We must contact the Assembly to awaken the Alpha spirits within the Alpha mortals, and we lack the power alone, especially confined to Mount Olympus."

Zeus continued to stare at the now clear mist floating at his feet on the dais, while he thought. He hadn't spoken to his father, Cronus, since he and his Olympians defeated and exiled the ruling Titans from Earth, and now Cronus was a member of the Assembly on their home world.

The Olympians had sealed their own fate when they expelled the ruling Titans back to the home planet, Titan, but that was before they discovered their terrible mistake. By interbreeding with mortals they had inadvertently corrupted the delicate controlling balance of the immortal Titan's Alpha and Omega souls (beginning and end) (good and evil) in all future mixed bloods, thus dooming Earth's population to an ever increasing and conflicting separation of spirits and ultimate goals in both the immortal and mortal races.

He refocused when Artemis began to speak. She had always been one of his favorites and always loyal and supportive. Artemis, his daughter and twin sister to Apollo, also shared a seat with the gods. His twins were born to Leto and not his wife and sister Hera, which is a major reason he protected them...to aggravate his wife.

Artemis said, "My father, my Zeus, I must agree with my brother and the others. This is what the Assembly exiled us to do. They are as much afraid of the potential power of an uncontrolled Omega as we are. No one can know the extent of their power if they are allowed to fully awaken and consolidate, and all of us knows only Alpha can stop them. The Assembly will not refuse; like us, they have no choice. They will help us awaken the dormant, immortal spirit of the Alpha residing in the mortals. It works to their advantage as well."

He knew Artemis was correct. It was just that he was the new supreme ruling god on Earth when he last spoke to Cronus, and Cronus would certainly remember the lightning bolts he had welded and launched at the Titans to drive them off this world.

Now, without the Titan's help the Olympians were stuck here in exile for eternity. Artemis was also right that the Titans also feared the awaking power of the Omega. That growing force would be totally unpredictable, extremely powerful and totally evil, and would eventually be able to challenge the Assembly on Titan. Yes, the Assembly would help, but still, he would now have to humble himself to them and ask for their help. So be it; he would pay the price.

"Very well. Project your thoughts with mine and let's reach out to Titan and the Assembly"

He felt the electric tingle of the charging power as their minds merged, focusing to project their joint mind. Then he felt the jolt, akin to an electric shock, as their joint minds streaked in unison across the cosmos. In the viewing mist of the dais they watched the stars flash past in the vast darkness of space. Their speed began to slow as they approached their goal, and soon they observed the planet Titan growing in the mist, filling the viewing mist. The view began to focus in on the planet and expand further. Titan's Mountain of the Gods then continued to expand to view the Assembly circled around their own viewing dais. They apparently had been monitoring his Olympian Assembly, because the appearance of the Olympians' forms did not seem to surprise them. Even so, the Assembly remained immobile and silent and continued to stare at them, obviously waiting for him to speak first. This arrogant statement of Titan's power angered him, but he held his anger, staring back into each pair of the assembled god's cold piercing eyes. After an excessively long pause Zeus said, "It is time. The Omegas are awakening, and the Alphas yet remain dormant." He left his statement brief, letting that fact sink in.

Hyperion, the Supreme Ruler of Titan, spoke, "Yes, we have been monitoring the situation on Earth, and we too find the situation grave. We don't understand why only the Omegas are awaking and the Alphas remain dormant. We suspect that an outside force is behind awaking only the Omegas spirits. It's like they are already organized with a leader. Do you think Hades could be behind it?"

That question shocked him. Mount Olympus had not heard from Hades since the war began against the mix-breeds. He and his Assembly had assumed Hades had been killed in that war, since he hadn't returned to his throne, but hearing Hyperion speak the words out loud, he realized that Hades could very well be behind it. He was a little surprise that he and the other Olympians had never considered that possibility, but he was not about to admit that fact. Hades had always caused problems on Earth; the chaos would give him strength. He responded, "We have no information to confirm that, but it is possible."

Cronus spoke to the Assembly saying, "Zeus and his Olympians caused the problem. It is their problem to solve. They assumed the responsibility when they took control of Earth!"

Hera was first to respond and blasted back, "You and the other Titans that were on Earth are just a guilty of fornicating with the mortal women. It's your problem, too!"

For once he was pleased with Hera's vicious verbal attack, since, for once, it was not directed at him. He almost wished she would take the form of a serpent, as she often did, to accent the venom of her words, but her verbal attack alone worked to silence Cronus.

Hyperion quickly seized the moment of silence to assume control again. "It has already been decided that we will help. We will begin radiating a mental stimulus toward Earth that will awaken the Alpha spirits and powers. Hopefully, it will not awaken the Omega further than they already are. It will take three rotations of the planet to fully saturate all the mortals, but you will have to act quickly to save them, because the Omegas will also be able to easily identify them as they awake by their auras. If, as you say, Omega is partially awake, this action will make any Alphas an easy target."

Zeus did not thank the Assembly, however he bowed slightly as his Assembly of gods withdrew and raced back across the cosmos to Mount Olympus. He thought it went well. At least no physical attacks were launched by either side. Now safe, he allowed the charge to slowly dissipate from his barely controlled lightning bolts, filling the chamber with bristling kinetic energy.

As they settled again into their adorned chairs surrounding the dais, Ares said, "Well, that wasn't so bad...no one died."

Zeus noticed signs of a general physical relaxation among the others, as if they had all been tensed for battle. He even noticed Apollo leaning his golden bow against his chair. He hadn't noticed Apollo with it at the Titan Assembly, but it stood to reason, since his bow had always been Apollo's weapon of choice and a constant adornment.

Ares continued, "Zeus, what do you think about Hyperion's suspicion that Hades might be behind the Omegas early awakening?"

"I saw Hades fall in the last battle. His body is dead." Zeus said, "But it's possible his soul might have survived. I think it could be possible that his spirit might still live within one of his descendant's mortal body. If so, his evil yet lives and has been refined by the corruption of the mortal bodies through hundreds of generations. Yes, Hades IS probably responsible for the Omegas' awakening, at least the corrupted part of his Titan spirit."

"What are we going to do about it, father?" Ares said.

"What we have been charged to do: correct the mistake. We must kill all the mixed-bloods, like we tried to do before, like we did to our own, Dionysus, but we must make sure we kill the corrupted Titan spirits, the Omega."

Hera screamed, "You wouldn't have had to kill your own son if you hadn't fornicated with that mortal harlot, Semele!"

At this interruption Zeus pointed a finger toward Hera, and a bolt of energy shot toward her, pinning her quivering body back in her throne. Zeus bellowed, "Silence! Semele was a princess!" None of the other gods moved or made a sound, fearing Zeus' wrath. As if nothing happened, Zeus continued, "Once the energy transmission begins we must monitor Earth continuously, seeking out the awakening Alphas and bring them here. They will be trained here to become our army against the Omega."

***

Mojo sat in his fifty story penthouse apartment and office surrounded by large screen televisions and monitors tuned to every major news feed from around the world. It looked like a control center in a major network headquarters, but it was all controlled, operated and monitored by his staff solely for him. In his many lifetimes he had spent at least one lifetime in all the major countries, so language was no barrier to him. Nothing important escaped his notice.

So when the news broke about the rare solar flare activity he actually laughed out loud. He felt the energy transmission even before the imbecile, human scientists announced to the world that the slight bluish shift in the visual spectrum of light was due to an extremely rare sunspot phenomena. He recognized it and knew exactly what it was: a declaration of war!

The Olympians, with apparent help from the Titans, were obviously attempting to activate the Alpha portion of the Titan spirit in an attempt to save them from extinction and fight back against his army of Omegas, but he was ready for them. It was far too late for the Alphas. He and his kind had spent thousands of years and many human generations purging the Alpha spirit from the Titan soul. Each transfer of the immortal Titan soul at the death of its human host corrupted the soul further and purged more of the Alpha from the Omega. Now after centuries each side of the soul was refined and virtually pure in its Alpha or Omega

12

human host, but only Omega was awake and organized. He had seen to that in secret. And they had been killing the Alphas on sight for centuries.

Mojo had been totally aware and fully awake in his Titan spirit for centuries and had transferred through many human bodies. His Omega spirit, being self-aware, had given him the advantage. He recognized the other Omega souls and had concentrated his combined spirit by carefully killing many of the human hosts and absorbing their Omega spirit into himself. Now none of the other Omegas possessed even close to his level of power. He allowed his commanders to also concentrate power but never allowing any one to be strong enough to challenge him. That could never be allowed.

Mojo had built a vast amount of Earth wealth through his concentration of his Omega power and living many human lifetimes. He gathered his fellow Omegas into his organization and controlled them with iron will and fists. His organization had infiltrated world corporations and governments and silently ruled many from his penthouse. He actually owned the high-rise building in Manhattan, New York and two more identical facilities in Moscow, Russia and Tehran, Iran. In point of fact, each headquarter was owned by him and all named the "Rose Building", which housed the corporate offices of his many corporations, along with the offices of his minions of Omega commanders. The key word, "Rose" was there for all to see, if they only looked, but the significance of the word indicated the headquarters of Omega. The Rose

Building and rose logo, with its red aura, served to attract the awakening Omega spirits to him.

To the outside human world he was unimpressive in looks, being purposefully average and plain. There was nothing to make him stand out. He looked like any other business executive in a three-piece suit. That is unless you happen to be a descendant of a Titan housing an active Alpha or Omega spirit. Then you would see his invisible Omega aura radiating from and encompassing him. Then you would fear him, for his huge, demonic red aura resembling a winged, two-headed, fire breathing dragon towered over him.

Mojo's ancient, long-range plans were quickly coming to fruition. Like a chessboard, all the elements were in place for world domination. His only remaining obstacles were the Olympian gods and remaining morphed Titan Alpha spirits. The Olympian gods didn't pose much of a problem directly, because the Titan immortals had been imprisoned by the Titan Assembly to remain isolated in Mount Olympus. While the Olympian gods couldn't travel to Earth, they could direct and work through the emerging Alphas through their human host. Things were going well for Mojo, and his only remaining concern was this potential Alpha intervention.

Through antiquity the Alpha spirit had always served as a balancing deterrent to prevent the Omega side of the Titan soul from becoming dominant. This balance made the immortal Titans who they were, body and spirit. This had all changed once the immortals began reproducing and mixing with the mortal humans. This genetic mix corrupted the balance of Alpha and Omega, allowing them to begin separating. It had taken several generations of the short-lived human mix-breeds before the Titans recognized what was happening. By then it was too late to stop it. Fear grew with this understanding, knowing what the ultimate outcome of the separation of the Titan soul. The Olympian Titans attempted to correct the problem by waging war on all mixed-bloods, attempting to kill the corrupted soul before the two sides could separate. The war failed miserably, because the entire human population rose up against the Titans. The humans did not understand the problem of the Titan soul and believed the Titans were attempting total genocide against all humans, and the humans fought back, forcing the Titans to vacate Earth, all but the Olympian gods left in exile, but they had to hide Mount Olympus, only the Olympians knew where.

Mojo had also recognized what was happening and saw the opportunity to take advantage of the situation and take control. He fed on chaos and misery, and the weak humans were fertile ground to spread both. He was not Mojo in the beginning. He had been called Hades back then, brother to Zeus, but by concentrating the Omega spirits into himself, he became far more powerful than Hades had ever been. Now he was Mojo, and all will fear.

Since he left Mount Olympus he had gone by many names such as Nero, Attila the Hun, Ivan the Terrible of Russia, and many others. He had murdered and tortured millions. By the 1700s he learned he could create more chaos in politics when he became Maximilien Robespierre and led the

French revolution. Then he learned that controlling governments and politics should be his ultimate goal.

Now Omegas' separation was complete and almost free to exercise their combined will, his will, over the dwellers of this planet, Mount Olympus and eventually Titan as well. Soon Omega would enslave the humans and Titans, and, as their leader, he would become the Supreme God of all, the most powerful throughout the cosmos. All they had to do to realize his plan was finish off the Alpha; they were the only force in the universe that could potentially stop them. Alpha had the knowledge, potential power, and inherent hate to battle Omega. Now with this Titan energy ray, the dormant Alpha would awaken and be able to fight back. All the centuries of waiting was now over. The war had begun.

They had already found and killed thousands of the dormant Alpha. Their weak auras was the signature of the dormant Alpha. Now, with the awakening of the Alpha spirits their auras would be easier to see. All Mojo had to do was send his army out across the world, seeking out those few remaining auras.

Until now, the only obstacle they have had has been the human police. They didn't understand the nature of the battle and the necessary mutilation of the human body housing required to destroy a Titan soul. Out of necessity his demon army has had to restrict their attacks to non-populated areas or the dark of night, but they had been quite successful in destroying many Alphas. Their victory would be complete when all Alphas had been destroyed.

16

# Chapter 2
# Dark Angels Unite

Jessica worked as a secretary/receptionist at a large real-estate agency in downtown Charlotte, North Carolina, at least until four days ago. When the strange sunspots activity began, at least that is what the news announced, she experienced a severe headache and apparently delusional episodes. It was the worst headache she had ever experienced, but, more disturbing, everything took on a bluish hue, and she began seeing things that couldn't possibly be there.

As she sat at the reception counter nursing her headache and staring out at the passersby, suddenly she saw four men approaching in the crowd that appeared to have a bright red aura around them. Upon closer inspection, the auras took on the shape of ... of ... what she could only call demons. The auras had rams horns wrapped around either side of their heads, long snouts full of teeth, ghoulish. The hands were large with long, sharply pointed claws that swung at their sides like pendulums at the end of large and longish arms. She tapped her coworker, pointed and said, "Do you see that, those four strange guys"

"What? What guys?"

Pointing, as they walked by the front window, she said, "There!"

"The only thing strange is that they are wearing identical trench-coats," the coworker said.

Jessica was feeling very strange. Not only did she see the apparition, but she felt ... evil radiating from them. It frightened her, and it enraged her at the same time. She thought, What the hell is going on here? Am I going crazy?

Jessica quickly told her friend that she was too sick to stay, and that she was going home. She didn't wait for a response and quickly gathered up her belongings and slipped out the front door. Once there, she peeked around the recess of the building to follow the four men as they continued down the sidewalk at a fast pace. They did not look back, so she briskly followed, continually ducking in and out of recesses along the block. As she continued down the block, she suddenly saw the focus of their attention. About half a block ahead of the four she saw a man with what appeared to be a bright golden aura surrounding him. The man, apparently aware of the others, began to run. He obviously was afraid and kept looking back over his shoulder as he ran. The four immediately broke into a run in pursuit.

Just as she was about to follow, she unexpectedly saw her own reflection in one of the office windows and stopped in her tracks to stare, open mouthed, at her own reflection. Surrounding and encompassing her reflected body image was a bright golden aura in the shape of a great owl, complete with outstretched wings. What the hell! She quickly looked around and saw that none other in the crowd of pedestrians had an aura, and no others seemed to notice hers.

She certainly didn't understand, but she again turned her attention to the four running men/demons in time to see them turn down a side street. She didn't see the other golden aura identified earlier, but she assumed he had also turned down the side street. She must find out what this craziness was all about, so she continued forward, now also running. She reached the side street in time to see the four men turn into an alley. Jessica, scared but curious, cautiously approached the alley and peered around the corner. The man with the golden aura was now petrified in fear. He had run into a dead-end alley, which was now blocked by the four men, approaching and spreading out to prevent his escape. As she watched the four men/demons opened their trench-coats and pulled out swords ... SWORDS! She watched in horror as the four demon men converged on the frightened man and began to mutilate the man in the golden aura ... like hers! At some point during the mutilation of the man's body, the golden aura faded and ceased to exist.

Trembling, she shrank back around the corner of the alley and ran for her life. She had to hide from these men. Who were they? Hell, it didn't matter; they apparently wanted to kill her, too. She had been lucky, very lucky. What if they had found her first? She wouldn't know what was happening until it was too late, like that poor man. He could hardly know their intentions, and had died a horrible death.

Jessica hailed the first cab she saw. She wanted to get out of the public and sight and get home as quickly as possible, so she could consider all these new occurrences. She had to think!

On the way home she slumped in the taxi seat to keep from being seen, but she kept popping her head up to survey the crowd. There were no other auras to be seen en route to her apartment, and she was thankful. Certainly, the four demons weren't chasing her, and if she was lucky, they hadn't seen her at all.

She quickly locked up her apartment and closed all her shades. Even so, she knew she wasn't safe if the four demons wanted in. Jessica had seen what the demons were capable of, and a simple door would only slow them down. For a moment she thought about calling the police, but what would she tell them? How could she explain about the demon auras? Apparently, she wouldn't be able to show them hers either. Calling the police seemed like just asking for an invitation for a visit from other men in white coats.

Thinking about the aura reflected in the store window she had seen surrounding her, she quickly went to her mirror to see if it really existed. Staring back at her big as life hovered her golden aura. The great owl's golden piercing eyes seemed to stare directly into her own blue eyes. They watched each other, but this time there was something strangely familiar about the aura, something she couldn't quite remember, like the memory was there, just slightly out of reach.

Pondering this latest development, she made her way to the kitchen and made herself a stiff drink; she didn't care what as long as it had alcohol in it. If ever she needed a drink, today was the day. But, before relaxing she detoured into the bedroom to retrieve the .38 pistol from the nightstand that she kept for self-defense. If ever she needed defense, today was also that day.

Now relatively safe and feeling the relaxing effects of the orange juice and Vodka, she began to relive the unbelievable events of the day. None of it made sense, but as she went through the day, she suddenly realized that one of her kind, whatever that was, died at the hands of the demons today. Again, she watched in her mind as that golden aura had faded away as the horrified man was literally sliced apart in bloody pieces, falling in every direction. This filled her with a seething rage, a rage so intense she couldn't comprehend. She actually wanted to search for them and kill them. How insane was that?

After a fitful night's sleep, the next day started with a call in to her office telling them she was still sick. She wasn't sure what to do, but she certainly wasn't going out. She peered out the window shades often to scan the people passing by, but there was never a sight of any auras and began to doubt that she had ever seen anything. No, she wasn't crazy. She had definitely witnessed the murder, and later in the day the television began to confirm the grisly death of some man. They gave his name and some facts about him. He was some bank teller or such, not a mobster as she had tried to rationalize, but he was more. He was the man with the golden aura ... like hers.

Jessica began to slowly remember bits of other things...another life, an ancient life, even multiple lives. They were bits and pieces of lives and powers, fantastic powers, but her thoughts were so jumbled. She had had another name back then, long ago at the beginning. It came to her in a flash, like a slap to the face; her name had been Athena, and she had worn a white toga with a golden belt. She had also worn a golden crown. It seemed so real, that life.

Jessica quickly came back to her senses by a loud knock on her door. She rushed to the door and peered through the peep hole. Instant panic froze her at the sight of bright red auras outside her door. There were men outside, but all she saw were the auras. Thinking quickly, she said, "Who is there?" She then ran to the coffee table for her .38.

A man from the other side said, "We are from the gas company. There was a gas leak outside your office yesterday, and we heard you were sick. We came by to check on you."

She knew there was no getting out of this. There were four large men outside against her, barely 5' 4" and 120 pound body. She had no chance, but she turned surprisingly calm and feeling stronger by the second, as a calming power seemed to be flooding her body. She said, "I'm fine."

The man said, "We must check you out. Please open the door."

She faced the door with her gun cocked and said, "Hell no! Go away!" As soon as she spoke, the door exploded inward, followed immediately by the four demons bursting inside brandishing their swords. Something seemed wrong, though. They seemed to move in slow-motion, but she didn't waste time considering it. She took careful aim and shot each one in the head as they spread out. The men fell dead at her feet, but the angry demon auras continued to snarl and snap at her. The auras finally floated free from the dead bodies and drifted away, obviously still alive. Then she remembered the golden aura and how it dissolved and died when the demons had severed the man's head and body. Only now did she realize the significance of the swords. The demons' intent was to kill her aura as they had the man's, and of course her body too in the process. Some of this was beginning to make sense; swords killed the aura if you dismember the body.

Jessica's mind was very clear and working well. With the realization that her life had permanently changed, she knew she would never be able to stay here or ever have a normal life again. Also, with the realization that she had little time, she took one of the swords and sheath for her own use and hid it under her mattress. She then went through the pockets of the four men and removed a substantial amount of cash, which she also hid. This would be her expense money. Then she waited appearing as a helpless victim for the neighbors and police to come.

The police had no problem calling this a home invasion and justified self-defense killings. If you bust someone's door down in North Carolina, you kind of expect to get shot, especially if you are a gorgeous, young, blonde female. Sadly, however, they took her .38 as evidence. They had many questions, but the men were unknown to her, and she wasn't about to tell them about the auras or the murder she had previously witnessed. They would probably lock her up as being crazy.

After what seemed like hours, they all let her go and drifted away, but as soon as she was alone, she retrieved the sword and strapped it on her back then covered it with her own black, leather trench-coat. She had to leave and hide somewhere, and quickly.

Earlier, when the crowd was thickly gathered, she had noticed another lone red aura at the peripheral of the crowd. It must have seen her earlier when she left her office and followed her. It made no attempt to come close, but obviously it knew she had survived, and it would be summoning others. She had to hide.

Previously, in her haste to catch a cab to escape the demons, she had left her car at work. She now took a cab and retrieved it but remained extremely cautious. She rightfully believed, however, that there would be a small window of safety, while the next team of demons were en route.

On the outskirts of town she spent the night in a rickety, old motel that took cash and where she could hide her car. She didn't know how sophisticated the demons might be and was afraid to use credit cards.

Early the next morning she did three things: withdrew all her savings, traded her car in for a used black van with tinted windows, and left town. If the demons wanted her, they would have to find her, and she wasn't going to make that easy.

Buying the van was a second thought. Initially, she just wanted to get rid of anything that could be traced to her, but when she noticed the van, she hoped to be able to hide her aura inside the van and live out of it if necessary. The fact that the van was black was a plus. For some reason, possibly from her awakening memories, she was drawn to black.

The next morning's dawn found Jessica asleep in her van at a rest stop on I-24 just east of

Nashville, Tennessee, having driven late into the night. By midmorning she was shopping in a goth store in downtown Nashville. The draw of black leather was just too strong, and she surrendered to the urge. Soon she was decked out in black leather gloves, a short skirt, halter top and knee-high boots, all black leather; but it felt right to her. Her life may have changed, but if she was going out, it would be on her terms and dressed the way she wanted.

***

At the age of 67 Augustine (Augie) Turner was the newest socialite in Nashville, and she was bored. She had worked all her life and worked hard. Her and her husband started a software and computer company and built it into a multi-million dollar company. The effort required precluded having children; there simply wasn't enough time. Then, time ran out for her husband, who died two years earlier. After that she lost interest in the business and recently sold it for an obscene amount of money. Augie lived alone in a large older house near downtown Nashville. Now the ha-te-ta socialites wanted her company. Truth be known, all they wanted was her money and influence, but she had absolutely no interest in them or their activities. She had the money to do anything she wanted, but unfortunately, she didn't want to do anything.

Her personal dilemma recently took a back-seat to the flu. She had been in bed for the last three days with nausea and headaches, but today she finely felt well enough to eat something and clean up. That's when her troubles really began, and she knew she was a lot sicker than she thought.

After her shower she was drying herself in front of the vanity mirror, then she saw it. The room was foggy from the shower, but she noticed the golden glow lighting the room. As the fog cleared the glow slowly took the shape of a golden bear surrounding her, even when she moved. It startled her, but it wasn't threatening. Still, she realized she must be sicker than she thought. It couldn't be real, and she vowed to call the doctor about it. Maybe he could give her some medication to get her head straight.

With her improving health she was beginning to feel a little stir-crazy, being locked up in her house, and decided to get out and go for a walk. What the hell else could she do with no business demands. So far in her life, except for this bout with the flu, she still had her health, and it was about time to take advantage of it before it left her.

Although she lived in a quiet residential area, it was only a few blocks to an active business street. She decided to walk the business section. Maybe feeling this business pulse might help bring her out of this depression.

Soon she found herself window shopping on the busy business street and was startled to again see her golden bear hovering over her reflected in the window. She had forgotten about it and thought, It's not real. But, also reflected in the window was another glow coming from across the street, two actually. On closer examination she saw that both glows were red and menacing and staring directly at her, then she noticed that the golden bear seemed extremely agitated. This frightened her. What if these auras are real?, she thought. She tried to act nonchalant and began heading back home.

Augie knew they must be real and that she was in serious trouble when the red auras began to follow her.

***

On her way back to the interstate, Jessica suddenly braked and veered to the curb. Just a block ahead were two demons. They hadn't seen her, being intent on their quarry ahead. Following the demons' focus, she saw a bright golden aura ahead surrounding a woman that looked to be in her mid-sixties. From the last experience she knew the woman was doomed. Well, without her help the woman would be doomed, but she had no intention of allowing them to kill this woman and aura, not again.

Jessica's persona reverted and she was now Athena the goddess warrior. She felt the change again flush over her and the power surge within her. The hunters were now the hunted, as she sank into the shadows to survey the crowd. There were no other demons, that she saw, so she resumed the hunt. The older woman had yet to see the demons, or acted as if she hadn't. Would the woman be able to see the demon aura? Would she even feel a need to look back or suspect danger? Possibly not. The demons had gotten closer but were apparently waiting for her to take them away from the crowd of pedestrians and shoppers, which she now did by turning off on a side street. Athena knew they would strike when the woman reached the alley. Athena didn't wait and drew her sword from under her trench-coat and ran toward their backs. She reached them just as the demons grabbed the woman and roughly pushed her into the alley.

27

The woman was screaming for help, but Athena was louder saying, "Leave her alone!" The diversion worked, and the demons temporarily forgot the woman and spun around to face her armed with their swords. They charged her, but as before, they appeared to be moving in slow-motion, and she easily sidestepped and parried their sword swings. They, however, were far too slow to move away from her attacks. Her swings were not even defended, and Jessica took off both heads quickly and cleanly, but just in case, she continued. As the demons had destroyed the man before, so did she. The mutilation of both demons came quickly. She had no remorse, in fact, she struck with pent up rage and ferocity she did not know she had. As she lopped off the heads, the red aura evaporated, withering in death, death of the men and demon auras.

Again, Jessica quickly emptied the pockets of the demons of their rolls of hundred dollar bills, then turned to the dazed woman asking, "Are you all right?" In shock, the woman ignored her. Jessica quickly stepped close and slapped the woman hard and said again, "Are you OK?"

"Yes, thank you, but what just happened?"

"There's no time for that. We have to get out of here. Follow me." Jessica took her arm and led her out of the alley and back toward her van. She tried not to draw any attention to themselves, but the woman was shaky and stiff. They finally reached the van, and she got the lady inside and quickly left the area. At the first safe, convenient location she pulled into a parking lot, locked all the doors and went to the back to comfort the shaken woman.

The woman looked intensely at her and said, "You saved my life. Thank you." Then after a moment she continued, "Why were they trying to kill me?"

Jessica wondered how could she explain something that she herself hardly knew. Then she asked, "Did you see the demon aura around them?"

The woman sighed in relief and said, "Oh, thank God. I thought I was going crazy and imagining it. Yes, it scared the crap out of me. I see an aura around you, also. What the hell is going on here?"

"I am not really sure myself," she said. Jessica went on to describe her activities of the last couple of days in detail, hoping that maybe the woman might offer some answer or make some sense of it. Jessica finished the story by telling the woman how she had spotted the demons and followed them down the side street in time to save her. "I know that sounds unbelievable, but it is all true. I am running, trying to hide, and I think maybe you had better come with me, because whatever this aura is, you have it too." Jessica noticed that it was in the shape of a golden bear. "They will come for you again."

The woman listened intently without interruption or expression, and it was hard to know what she was thinking, if anything. Jessica waited for her response.

Finally, the woman said, "That is a fantastic story. It is hard to believe. No one else would believe, but I must believe, because I have seen the

29

demon auras. I have seen my own aura, and I am looking at yours right now. Somehow we apparently have a kin-hood of some kind. I think you are right. We must stick together, and try to figure this out. What do you suggest?"

"I really don't have a plan," Jessica said. I was mostly headed away from Charlotte. The demons will be looking for me there. Now the demons will be looking for you here in Nashville. I suppose we could head to St. Louis, at least they shouldn't be looking for us there."

"By the way, my name is Augustine, but I go by Augie."

"Nice to meet you, Augie. My name is Jessica ... I think. My name might be Athena, too." Jessica took her first really good look at the lady. Augie stood about 5' 7" and was older with grey hair, but she could tell she had been a looker in her younger days. She still had a nice body for her age and beautiful blue eyes that looked deep into you.

Augie continued, "I suppose it is too dangerous to go by my home? I live alone and nothing is stopping me from leaving, but it might be nice to get a few personal things, maybe some cash, and I need to call my attorney. I am filthy rich you know, and if I just vanish, people will be looking for me, and we don't want the police helping the demons find us. I also have some pistols for self-defense there we might could use."

At first Jessica started to say no, but then she realized it would take a little time for the other demons to discover their missing and dead companions. En route to Augie's house Jessica offhandedly said, "The pistols can be used in emergencies to save our lives, but shooting the body only kills the body, and the aura gets away, presumably to control another body. The only thing that kills the demon aura apparently is chopping off the head, at least it killed those last two that way." This brought a startled look from Augie.

Augie said, "I'm not sure I could help you much in a sword fight, but maybe I can keep them off your back, even if I have to shoot them. Maybe I can wound them."

Jessica said, "Just don't shoot me!" This brought a hearty laugh from both.

They spent the night in a motel in the suburbs of St. Louis, not really knowing what they would do next. As they were readying to leave, Augie stiffened and stood immobile. As Jessica looked at her, wondering what was wrong, it seemed Augie's eyes were unfocused and her mind was somewhere else.

After a moment Augie said, "There is another one of us in trouble. I feel her fear in my mind, and I know where she is ... I think. Let's hurry!"

***

Azlana had been sick in bed for days, having missed classes and a mid-term test at the University of Missouri Saint Louis, thank God for basketball scholarships. This was unusual for her, as she was never sick. Her head hurt terribly ever since the sunspot activity started, and she wished it would hurry up and go away. She had taken all the aspirin in her apartment and reluctantly decided to get up and walk to the drug store on the corner for more. As she staggered into the bathroom to comb her hair, she stopped abruptly, frozen, staring at her reflection in the full-door mirror.

Staring back at her from the mirror was the customary chocolate brown face, lean, muscular body, and dark eyes; but also staring back was a golden image of an angry looking black panther hovering over her and completely encompassing her body. She spun around to see if it was behind her, but nothing was there. She returned her gaze to the reflection, and it was back. The dazzling bright fangs and claws were bared, telegraphing danger. But the most striking feature of the panther was the eyes; they shone with a fiery intensity, electric as a lightning bolt charging its energy to strike.

After the initial shock, it no longer frightened her. In truth, it looked like she felt at the moment ... intense rage. The translucent image hovered like a mist or aura, and it mirrored her movements. It was obviously part of her, but she didn't understand why or what it was. But admittedly, she kind of liked it.

She would have to figure it out later. Right now the throbbing in her head needed drugs, so she got herself dressed and presentable for public and left for the corner pharmacy. She cautiously stepped out on the sidewalk, prepared to run back in if anyone screamed at her aura, but none of the passersby reacted at all. The aura was still visible to her in the store windows she passed but apparently not to others, so she continued.

As she was starting to leave the store, again she stopped in her tracks, staring. Across the street was another aura, but this one was angry red, and the image was horrible looking, almost demonic. It was staring right at her. Oh crap, she thought. She saw the hate and rage in the demonic aura figure, but more surprising was the fact that she also felt hate and rage for it. She had seen this image before, long ago in distant memories, but she couldn't remember where or when. It had frightened her before but not this time. Now it was like a releasing... releasing her rage.

It looked as if it was waiting for her to come out, and its intentions certainly weren't friendly. Fortunately, however, he did not know who he would be messing with. Although still young, she had been raised in a rough neighborhood and knew how to take care of herself.

She returned to the pharmacy and exited out the back door, taking with her the steel locking bar for the door. She placed the steel bar against the wall at the head of the alley, then quickly circled back to the pharmacy and out the front door, where she appeared to ignore the man and his demonic aura and casually walked around the corner. She could feel the evil following her. When she reached the alley she darted around the corner and grabbed the bar, waiting. As he rounded the corner, she caught him in the chest with the bar, and he went down like a fallen tree. The sword he brandished had gone unnoticed until it fell with a clank to the pavement. "Damn, that bastard really was trying to kill me," she said out loud.

The man was trying to get up, but Azlana bent down and picked up the sword and swung it, sending his head rolling. She said, "I told you you didn't know who you were messing with." The red aura faded to obscurity.

33

Slowly she craned her head around the corner to see it if was clear. It was definitely not clear! Two more of the demonic aura men were coming around the corner. Two to one was not good odds, so she clutched the sword tighter and took off running down the alley. When she was halfway down the alley two more demon auras came into the alley from that end. Damn, she had hoped to die in bed at an old age.

She held her ground in the center of the alley, waiting for her inevitable death. The auras were approaching when suddenly a black van entered the alley and bore down on the last two red auras to enter. The van struck the two and knocked them rolling, as a petite blonde with a golden aura like hers jumped from the van and viciously attacked them as they tried to get up. Two more heads rolled from the blonde's sword, as Azlana turned to face the last two demons. They now approached slowly, seeming too slowly. Their movements and attacks seemed sluggish now, and she easily batted their slashes away with her sword, then struck so fast they offered no or little defense. It was almost too easy, but this wasn't sport; this was life and death. The little blonde now stood beside her and nodded her approval at the missing heads.

The blonde said, "We need to get the hell out of here! Hurry! Oh, and bring the sword."

Azlana did exactly that, but she also grabbed a second sword as they ran toward the van. Once inside a third woman, also with a golden aura, sped them down the alley and away to safety.

Jessica, as she called herself said, "This is Augie, and you can thank her for saving you. She sensed your mind and knew you were in trouble."

Incredible! So much was happening and way too fast. A moment ago she counted herself dead. Now, she was alive, saved by two others ... like her, golden auras and all. In addition, there was power she didn't understand at play. The enemy moved slow. Was that a power? Now, she was told that this lady, Augie, sensed her mind. Was telepathy another power? Azlana's mind was caught within a tornado of churning confusion, but surprisingly, her headache was gone.

Azlana said, "Well, what are we going to do now?"

"Hell if I know," Jessica said, "We are just running and hiding. You have any ideas?"

Azlana thought for a moment then said, "I know what's back there, so I'm going with you two, but there is one thing I want."

Augie said, "What's that?"

"I want to go shopping. If we are going to fight, I want some black leather like this little one." That's exactly what they did.

Afterwards, they drove west to put some distance between them and the demons, hopefully. After fifty miles or so they found a rest area on the interstate and pulled off, then found an isolated area where they could stretch and talk. Azlana was just beginning to formulate her questions when suddenly they all began to shimmer in a strange light. As she watched, they became translucent and flashed out of existence, only to reappear in a mist surrounded by strange looking, thrones and almost mythical appearing people sitting around the small arena where her group stood.

There were six men and five women sitting around the arena or dais; all wore white robes ... no, most wore togas of varying forms. The dais was centered in a large open room encircled with tall columns supporting a massive stone roof. The whole palace looked ancient, like Greek architecture she had seen in books. The man on the prominent stone throne wore a white pleated shirt that wrapped across the chest down to apparently tie behind his back. A wide golden belt wrapped his waist and held the top of what looked like a solid white, pleated kilt. On his feet was a pair of simple sandals with golden straps that wrapped his legs to above his calves. A golden garland or crown wrapped his head to delineate his supremacy in this group, but he needed none of this for Azlana to know he was in charge. He was impressive: tall, dark complected, and muscular. She thought he must be in his mid-thirties, because he sported a full curly, brown beard without a sign of gray; but his gleaming, blue eyes told a different story. The eyes spoke of ancient power and wisdom of the ages.

Next to this leader, king, or whatever, sat a man of similar stature and looks; however he was dressed far more modestly. In fact, his' toga crossed over only one shoulder, exposing his left shoulder and a massive and hairy chest. In his right hand he held a three pointed spear she believed was called a trident.

The woman to his right was blond haired and beautiful and almost completely covered in a white silken wrap. As Azlana followed the circle of

36

thrones around, something seemed to stand out for each one. One carried a golden bow and quiver of golden arrows. Another wore golden shoes with wings on them. All the women were beautiful beyond belief, and the men were gorgeous hunks. Geeze ... Who the hell ARE these people? she thought.

She took in the scene in seconds, but they remained silent and waited for a response.

***

Zeus was summoned. Apollo announced that they had found some Alphas, suggesting more than one. He hurried to the throne room in time to see two golden auras in an alley surrounded by four Omegas. Two of the Omegas were down already, evidently hit by a black chariot, ... vehicle. The small blonde attacked them and killed them quickly, while the tall, black woman Alpha engaged the remaining two Omegas. The Omega spirits were evidently destroyed by the Alphas, since the auras faded away. The Alphas then quickly got in the van and left the area. Zeus said, "Follow them and don't lose them. We will retrieve them at the first opportunity."

Already, he was proud of the first two Alphas they discovered. The Assembly had been searching for days, looking for Alphas. Unfortunately, the very few they found were too quickly killed. The Omegas were extremely organized and mobilized all over the world in search of Alphas, and they must be using advanced human technology to search for them. Undeniably, the Omega organization correctly interpreted the awakening energy beam and deployed its army of demons.

37

They continued to follow the van to a location downtown, where three golden auras emerged from the van. Yes, there were three Alphas, and he was pleased. On their own they were uniting and killing Omegas. Unfortunately, they ducked into a store before they could retrieve them.[1] After a lengthy wait the Alphas reemerged and quickly darted back to the van and were gone, driving west. Eventually, they pulled into some kind of park area alongside the road on which they were traveling and into a secluded area. As they all emerged from the van together and remained stationary, Zeus focused the gods' energy and latched onto them with their energy beam.

The three startled Alphas materialized in the mist of the dais and stared at the circled gods, then began to focus on him on the main throne. They said nothing, just waited.

As they surveyed him he was evaluating them, and what he noticed immediately was his daughter, Athena, at least Zeus immediately identified her dominant Titan soul as his first born and favorite daughter, lost in the last battle to purge Earth of its mixed inhabitants. Thank the gods her spirit had not been killed.

Athena was easy to identify by her bright golden, Alpha aura surrounding and encompassing her body in the shape of a great owl, complete with outstretched wings, which seemed to nervously stroke the air as she walked. Her Alpha spirit was unquestionably already active, or in the process of becoming active. Being so visible, Zeus was somewhat surprised that she had yet survived identification and destruction by the Omegas, but he

38

had already seen her kill two Omegas and presumably more, since she was still alive.

He then remembered again whom she was. She was Athena, and she would remember the ancient Titan powers she once had. Her human body was different, however. Like the original Athena, this one was a gorgeous blonde but was smaller and petite. This Athena was also a great warrior and, if possible, more intimidating. She was also disarmingly young but filled with an abundance of Alpha energy. The Alpha energy would give her speed, strength and agility to make up for her lack of size, and although small and petite, Athena was plainly a perfect warrior, complete to the sword slung on her bare back.

She stood defiantly facing him clad in black leather and belts, and very little of either. She was a combination of what Earth men would call a Playboy Bunny and mighty warrior. Her demeanor radiated confidence in all that she did, but her bright, intense, blue eyes sparkled with wonder, like a child with new toys. Athena was ready, and Zeus was wonderfully pleased with his daughter.

Zeus also recognized the tall black female, not by looks, but by the radiated Alpha energy of her dominant Titan spirit and the golden aura resembling an angry panther encompassing her. She was none other than Asteria, sister to Leto, the mother of his twins Apollo and Artemis. He remembered that he had once lusted after Asteria, but she had evaded his advances of seduction. The last he heard of her she had become an Amazon and was killed by his mortal son, Heracles.

Her Titan spirit had survived, living now within this tall, lean, muscular, Nubian beauty, also dressed in black leather that accented her lithe form. In addition to the black leather, she had embedded silver spikes in various areas of her attire...quite gothic in appearance and very intimidating. Asteria also sported a sword, actually two, crisscrossed on her also bare back. Even without the swords and battle leather, one look into her smoldering, black eyes told you she was a warrior. Her intense, dark eyes looked right through you but saw everything. Everything about her was intimidating, even her beauty.

Zeus did not recognize the third human's Titan spirit, but her golden aura was strong in the shape of a bear. She was undeniably a descendant of Titan blood, but she would be questionable as a warrior due to the age of her human host. There would, however, be a home for her.

Zeus noticed the similar pattern in dress and dark demeanor of the two lovely warriors. Although physically very different, they were quite alike in many ways. They were undeniably fierce and intimidating warriors and also beautiful. They were a welcome sight to behold. These angelic creatures would be the foundation of his army of avenging angels...his Dark Angels.

This appraisal had only taken seconds, but the three remained staring, waiting for his response. Zeus smiled at them, genuinely pleased, and said, "Welcome to Mount Olympus. I am Zeus and these," spreading his arms wide, "are the Olympian gods, the Assembly. We have brought you here

40

because you are descendants of our race, and you are in danger."

Jessica said, "What do you mean we are descendants of your race? How do you know this?"

Zeus responded, "I know this because of your auras. It is a Titan aura and characteristic of the Titan spirit or soul. I also know because I recognize you. You are my daughter, Athena. Tell me, do you recognize this place? You once ruled here at my side."

"Strange, but this place seems vaguely familiar, like in a dream, and I have recalled the name of Athena as my own in another ancient life," said Jessica

Zeus said, "Your spirit is ancient. We here are all ancient and immortal, and so are your spirits. This is what caused the problem in the beginning. The Titan race colonized Earth many thousands of years ago and began mixing with the mortal humans, because, as you can see, our races are very similar. But we and our souls are immortal, while the human lifespan and soul is finite. It took many human generations to discover that the Titan souls that passed to the next blood descendant generations were becoming corrupted by mixing the races, and the counter reacting balance of Alpha and Omega was losing its fragile equilibrium and beginning to separate."

"Hold on!" Augie said, "Where are all your aura?"

Zeus said, "That is a good question good lady. The answer is quite simply that our immortal souls are still joined with our original immortal bodies, and our Alpha and Omega spirits are still in

41

balance. When the spirit becomes corrupted auras take on the dominant spirit. Auras don't become visible until after a transfer and awakening. The awakening of your Titan souls just occurred."

Augie blurted, "You say Titans have been here for thousands of years and you are still in your original body?"

Zeus countered somewhat testily, "Yes, dear lady. That is what immortal means. We live on through the ages without end. Now let me continue."

"In the Titan race the spark of life or soul, never dies unless destroyed by a physical separation of the body containing the soul. Normally, this life force transfers at the untimely death of its host's body into another living Titan body, or in your case a distant Titan descendant. The Titan soul you now possess has passed from human generation to generation, but remains the same ancient soul."

"The basic psyche of our soul includes both good (Alpha) and evil (Omega) in a delicately balanced mix. Titans are aggressive and malevolent yet gentle and caring as a result of the conflicting motivations and emotions of the soul. The human soul is also a balance of good and evil, but the human soul does not transfer to another living human, where ours will move to a descendant. Fortunately for Titans, our bodies are also immortal, mostly eliminating the problem. In the mixed bloods the corruption continued through many hundreds of human, short-lived generations and has now completed the full separation of Alpha and Omega. By allowing the races to mix we have

42

inadvertently unleashed uncontrolled evil upon the human race, dooming it to destruction."

"As you have already discovered, the evil, Omega, is now trying to kill the Alpha, and if you haven't figured it out already, you three are Alpha. We are trying to save you and the other Alphas, because Alpha is the only force in the universe that can destroy the Omega. This is why the Omega demons are trying to kill you. You are a threat to them, their only threat, and if they are not stopped they will kill every Alpha and enslave the human population."

Azlana spoke up for the first time and said, "Well, what is to become of us?"

Zeus said, "Ahhhh, You will become my avenging army to destroy the Omega."

"What if we don't want to become your army", said Azlana.

"I'm afraid beautiful warrior that you really have no choice. As long as you are here in Mount Olympus you are safe, but Omega will never cease looking for you, and they will kill you if you try to live on Earth outside of this place. Another thing you will discover is that your Alpha spirit hates the Omega spirit. Its function has always been to control Omega. The evil of Omega will cause your rage to build up in you, forcing you to seek them out and destroy them. I'm sorry, but it is inevitable. What we hope to do here is help you remember who you are and teach you how to use your powers. By joining together as many as we can find, as you have already learned, your chances of survival improves greatly."

Jessica already felt the rage and knew Zeus spoke the truth and had already accepted her fate. Her questions were more functional when she said, "If there is an army of Omegas out there, I hope there are more Alphas than us three."

It pleased Zeus that his daughter seemed to accept her roll, and responded, "You three are the first Alphas we have found, but we will find more as we found you."

"Well, the three of us were almost killed before you found us. I suggest you look harder and quicker," Jessica retorted somewhat angrily.

Athena always had a quick tongue, but sometimes he liked that about her. In this case, however, she was right, but he chose to ignore her retort. He said, "You will be shown your quarters and will be summoned when we find other Alphas. Now rise out of the mist so we can begin our search again."

# Chapter 3
## More Angels

Leviathan had always been an angry man, being involved in more than his share of trouble, but over time he had learned to manage his anger through exercise. He worked out constantly, eventually turning this compulsion into gainful employment. Now he managed a gym and helped others with physical and weight training, his huge, finely honed body providing the motivation for the customers to take his instructions seriously. Due to his physical refinement and intimidating size, few argued with or confronted him, which helped him control his internal rage. Without a focus or target for his rage, he had little trouble controlling it.

All this changed three days ago when he walked by a mirror in the gym. He saw the golden glow and quickly turned to see an image of a bull surrounding him. There was nothing standing behind him. It only showed in the reflected image of the mirror. For the first time in his life that he could remember, he was frightened. No one in the gym seemed to notice, which puzzled him. Apparently he was the only one that saw it, and after a while he started feeling self-conscious of himself, like there must be something wrong with him. He had a small room on the premises in the back in which he lived and started spending more time there away from the other customers. He was trying to figure out what was happening.

After a few days he started losing his battle with his pent up rage. For some reason the rage he had controlled most of his life was building to a boiling point. On the fourth day he couldn't stand being cooped up anymore and took a long walk around town. The weather was beautiful in San Diego, California today, so he had walked several miles in the open, finding himself down by the waterfront. As he reached the railing he turned to watch a cruise-ship slide passed through the bay. He didn't know if it was coming or going, and it didn't really matter. The view was hypnotic, but as he suddenly turned, he noticed another glow, two actually, a few hundred feet behind him. They apparently had been following, because they also turned to the railing as if they too were watching the ship. The second thing he noticed was that they were wearing tan trench-coats, certainly not normal for San Diego weather; but it was the bright red glow of the translucent image of, hell if he knew what, something ugly and threatening, that got his attention. The eyes even glared at him with obvious hate.

What happened then was a blur. Leviathan completely lost control of his rage. It burst out in a snarl so menacing that the other pedestrians ran in every direction, but the effect on the ugly SOBs was more surprising. They evidently did not expect him to attack them both, but they quickly recovered and managed to pull swords from under their trench-coats as he ran toward them. By the time Leviathan reached them he was totally berserk. He tore into them as if they were children. The swords they tried to swing were easily batted away. He had a head clamped under each arm, as he slammed the heads together until they were mush. Once they stopped fighting he broke their bodies more and tossed them into the bay. The red glowing monsters continued to snap at him, but when he closed his fingers around their throats, his fingers passed right through. The glows drifted away, still snarling at him.

As his senses slowly came back to him, he looked around. Crowds of onlookers were standing around pointing, but what stood out from the crowd was a large group of about ten more of the red glowing monsters running toward him. They were still a block away, so he took off running like crazy. Ten of the devils were more than even he could defeat. He also heard sirens in the distance and realized the police were on the way. In their eyes he had just killed two men, no matter that they had swords and invisible monsters surrounding them. The police would shoot first and talk later. So, he ran even faster.

Leviathan's rational senses were alive again, and the situation didn't look good. Ten against one wasn't healthy odds, not to mention the police. The pedestrians and tourists had probably taken thousands of pictures, probably even a few videos as well. The police would find him soon enough, certainly if he went back to the gym, since he had the misfortune to have worn a T-shirt advertising his gym. His life was pretty much over either way, but still he needed to avoid the monsters right this moment.

Leviathan began a series of sprints, turning corners at random, trying to lose the small army of monsters. He didn't see them behind him and began to feel a little more comfortable right up to the instant he encountered the dead-end alley. Quickly turning, he took off back up the alley but didn't get far. Somehow the monsters had been able to track him, as if by satellite, because they apparently knew exactly where he was and spread out across the entrance to prevent his escape.

\*\*\*

Augie felt like she was on a roller-coaster ride of emotions and input ever since the augmentation ray began her awakening, but she loved the excitement. She felt like she was alive for the first time in her life. It was like, for the first time, she had a purpose, and that purpose was to kill the demons. It was a welcome feeling, and God knows she had the rage to do it. What she didn't have was the strength of youth like these kids. They were unquestionably magnificent warriors and suited for the task ahead, but, honestly, what could she do to serve the team? Still, she was a member of the team and this was welcome. She would not be denied this opportunity. Yes, she was in for the duration no matter what.

There must not have been any servants or worker, because one of the gods, she didn't know which one, took them to their separate quarters to settle in, but quickly Jessica, Azlana, and herself had congregated in her room to talk. In reality, they had sought her out. They seemed to want, almost need, her company, almost like a mother. She had never been a mother but welcomed the attention, however. Augie had never had time to have children. Her and her husband had built a business, which took all her time. Now she regretted it, and

48

almost welcomed the interaction and matronly responsibility.

With the realization of who and what they were, the kids were afraid, but they weren't about to show it. Augie was afraid also but for a different reason. She was afraid that she had nothing to contribute to the team and was fearful she might have to go back, or worse. From what she now understood about the Titan spirit never dying and transferring if the human host died, she thought the gods might kill her so her spirit could transfer to a younger descendant. Maybe that was best. She didn't want to be left out and have to remain in Mount Olympus, while they were sent to fight. That would almost be a fate worse than death.

Apollo had come to talk with them, explaining some of the dormant powers that needed to be awakened. During this conversation Apollo discovered that Augie had sensed Azlana's fear and used it to find her and save her. Augie needn't have worried about any lack of usefulness, because Apollo tested and informed her that her power of telepathy was strong and would be a valuable contribution. Augie was actually surprised how easily telepathy came to her. Apollo had also told her that her power to control time was also strong, and had instructed her in its use. Still, she didn't understand about controlling time but figured it would eventually come to her. She had seen it in action before, making the demons appear to be moving in slow-motion. Without knowing how Jessica must have used this power against the demons. Now, hopefully, Augie could wield this same power. Augie was ecstatic that she would be able to contribute to the team.

Since that meeting Apollo had communicated telepathically with her on several occasions, and used it now to summon them all to the throne chamber. Apollo said, "We have found another Alpha. We need you all at the dais, now!"

They quickly grabbed their weapons and rushed to the dais. As they entered they immediately saw in the mist of the dais a single golden aura trapped in a blocked off alley, and at the other end came ten of the red demon auras.

Zeus said, "Quickly, enter the dais and we will teleport you."

Talk about tossing us all into the heat of battle, but that is exactly what they did, as she led Jessica and Azlana into the mist.

For the second time they watched the sparkling energy encompass them and whisk them from the mist into the alley slightly in front of a huge man with the golden aura. Augie quickly said, "We came to help you." He stared at them for a few seconds, but evidently seeing their golden auras, accepted them as friends and nodded. The man had no weapon, so Azlana tossed him one of her swords, which he easily caught, and she said, "We will take flanking positions on either side of you. Let's go get them. Oh, and be sure to cut their heads off, or they will come back later in another body."

The three of them charged forward, like they had fought together all their lives, while she followed behind. Augie had her pistols, but they were only for back-up. Her contribution would be to alter and slow time to make the demons move slower, while the Alphas would appear to the Omegas as moving at fast-forward speed. Apollo had told her that, with practice, this time shift could be used to make them so fast that they could become invisible to the time altered observer, but she was unable to master that feat as of yet.

This huge man with the golden aura bellowed out his rage as he ran. She thought how appropriate that his aura was in the image of a raging bull, because he was charging like one.

As Apollo had shown her, she began her attack by concentrating on the demons and focusing her mental power, and it was working. The demons were also charging, but their movements slowed perceptibly. Her mental energy appeared to momentarily freeze the expression of horror on the demons' faces, which she almost found humorous, because the bellowing bull seemed to frighten the hell out of them. Being demons from hell, she thought that was appropriate.

The demons were slower, but their physical power had not diminished. A sword strike from the demons would easily kill any of the team, and the odds were over three to one. This engagement remained extremely dangerous. Nevertheless, the raging bull went through them like a juggernaut, ripping, slicing and kicking his way through them. As the demons were knocked to the side into the other demons, knocking them off balance, the girls made quick work of them. Six of the demons perished on the first pass, then the golden warriors had the demons blocked from escaping, which they were trying to do. The odds were almost even now, which of course meant the demons had no chance of escape or survival. The golden warriors began to taunt them, enjoying the fear they were generating in the demons, but they could hear the police sirens getting louder and finished the job just as the police cars turned into the alley, now blocking them. Then to the astonished police, the four of them began to shimmer and disappeared, leaving a carnage of bloody and headless bodies behind, and of course, the police couldn't see the melting and dying demon auras.

*\*\**

Zeus had a huge smile on his face as the warriors materialized in the mist. Not only had the warriors excelled against overwhelming odds, but as they became visible, he knew instantly that the man warrior spirit was of his son, Heracles, by a mortal woman. Although the impressive aura caught his attention, it was the powerfully muscular, human body that identified him so quickly. The body appeared almost identical to the body Heracles had in life. He was a superior warrior then, and, without question, few could match his physical attributes today.

Hera said, "I do believe this is a reincarnation of your bastard son."

"Damn you woman. Be silent," Zeus said with a stern look. Hera recoiled somewhat and remained silent.

Zeus then turned toward the golden bull aura and said, "Welcome, Heracles." The warrior looked around to see if he was talking to someone else. Seeing no one, he started to respond, but Zeus silenced him with his hand. Zeus continued, "Your fellow warriors will educate you soon. You will

52

then understand, but know this. The dominant spirit that gives you your golden aura has descended from my son, Heracles. I will address you as so, like I will address you all that have recognized dominant spirits. Pointing to each as he spoke, he said, "You are Heracles. The small blonde is Athena. The tall Nubian woman is Asteria." When he came to Augie he looked around at the other gods to see if any of them knew her spirit. None spoke, so he said with some authority, "And you are Augie." He then looked back at Heracles and asked, "Do you have any questions?"

Leviathan said, "Well, I guess I will learn from my new friends here just what the hell is going on, and if you want to call me Heracles, I will answer. All I know for sure is that after what happened today, I can't go back to my old life. These warriors told me this is home, so be it. But, I do have a favor to ask."

"What is that?"

Heracles said, I want to go shopping. I need a better and heavier weapon, and I want some black leather like these other warriors.

Augie spoke up and said, "If you like, I can take us shopping if you can send us back to the van where we hid it. I have money there, and I would like to buy some leather also. I can mentally speak to Apollo when we are ready to come back."

Zeus thought for a moment and said, "Very well." He thought it was a good idea for the warriors to spend time together, and he wanted them happy. Soon they were back in the black van on their way, but he insisted that the gods continue to monitor them for their own safety. He instructed them not to go back to St Louis, because the police were looking for them there, so drive to another big town before shopping.

***

Augie was somewhat surprised to find Jessica's van undisturbed, but it was remote and hidden. They decided to continue on toward Tulsa, Oklahoma. It was as good a place as any. Augie drove as the rest settled in for a long trip, and Jessica and Azlana began to catch Heracles up on all that had transpired, including each of their personal stories, including my own. Of course, I had much more life and history than any of them, but that past life didn't contribute much to this new life into which we had all been thrust.

It actually seemed natural to refer to the huge man as Heracles; it fit, and he seemed to easily make the switch. She thought he secretly liked it. They had never heard his real name anyway, and at this point it didn't matter much.

By the time they reached Tulsa they were long friends, fitting easily into each other's new lives and rolls. This camaraderie continued with the shopping. They found a goth store, and all helped Heracles with his choices. It was even fun. The girls had him all decked out in black leather and an abundant assortment of battle spikes; that was Azlana's contribution. It proved to be a little more difficult to find the weapon, but once he found it he immediately claimed it as his. It was a double-bladed battle-axe so heavy only he could wield it, but he could handle it easily with either hand if necessary.

54

They all laughed at his comment when he said, "If we need to chop off heads, what could be better?"

***

Susan (Sue) Macintosh was in the 7th grade at Holy Family Cathedral School in Tulsa, Oklahoma. It was a private Catholic school, but her family was wealthy and affluent and could easily afford it. Their wealth had something to do with oil; that's all she knew. Sue usually liked her school, but lately she had been afraid to go. It all started with the golden fog; it looked like an eagle around her. She saw it, but no one else could see it. When she told her parents they were concerned and even called a doctor to come check her out, but he told them that children sometimes have a vivid imagination and nothing was wrong, physically, with her. It wasn't her imagination; she knew it when she saw others with a red glow watching her at school. They looked hideous and scared her. Again, she told her parents, but they scoffed at it and wouldn't let her stay home from school. They told her she was safe, and if it weren't for the glowing men she would have felt safe. Her driver that took her to school and picked her up was also a bodyguard. But, every day for the last few days she had seen the men watching her at school, and she was really frightened.

Today, while she was eating her lunch outside and talking to some friends, the glowing men ran into the school yard and grabbed her. It was the same men that had been watching her, and this time she got a good look at the red glow. It was repulsive and monstrous. She screamed and fought

55

them, but they were strong and began to drag her away. Her friends began screaming and teachers and a guard came running. The monster men pulled large swords and forced them back. Sue knew then that she was about to die.

*** 

With their shopping done, Augie and the other Alphas were driving around through a residential area, still laughing and joking, when Heracles began to growl and stare out the window. His warning was just barely ahead of mine. I felt the distress in my mind. We were passing a middle-school at the time, and in the school yard stood two blazing red demon auras. Suspended between them was a small girl with flaming red hair, kicking and screaming. She appeared to be about twelve years old draped in a golden aura of an eagle. The demons were dragging her out of the yard, undoubtedly to be executed out of sight of the many witnesses. Other kids were pointing screaming and some teachers were trying to pull the men off, but the demons pulled their swords from under their trench-coats, forcing them back.

Heracles was out the door before she could get stopped and was running toward the demons. Jessica and Azlana were right behind him. The demons immediately saw them and dropped the girl and turned, growling, to face their ancient enemy. Jessica scooped up the girl and pulled her to safety, while Heracles charged in, swinging his axe. Augie had not been able to get there in time to alter time, but this power was already in play, and the demons were unable to maneuver out of the way.

Clearly, Jessica also possessed the power over time and didn't quite realize it yet. She would have to give Jessica some instructions, as Apollo had given her; although she seemed to be doing well.

Heracles' attack was without mercy, lopping off a demon's head and sending it rolling across the school yard, to the horror of those watching. On the back swing he caught the second demon deep in the side, sending him to the ground. Azlana sent the second head rolling. Both red auras slowly withered and vanished, as their vile screeching also slowly faded.

Jessica held the girl tight in her arms, and her little arms also wrapped tight around Jessica, comforting in her protection. Jessica said to the teachers, "This girl is in danger from forces you can't possibly understand. Neither the school or this girl is safe as long as she is here. We are taking her so she can be protected. Tell her parents she is now safe."

Augie was back behind the wheel as the warriors and the little girl entered the van. They sped off, taking many turns to avoid being chased by the police. Her only thought was to put as much distance as possible from Tulsa. By taking the little girl an Amber Alert would be generated immediately and everyone would be looking for them. Of course they had no choice if she was going to live, even the girl knew that. Seeing the golden auras, the girl immediately identified them as friendly and must have felt safe.

Azlana asked the girl, "Do your parents have a golden aura?

The girl, Sue, said, "No. I tried to tell them about my glow, but they didn't believe me, and they don't glow like you people do. I tried to tell them about the scary red glows of the men that have been watching me, but they didn't believe that either. I have been so frightened. Thank you for saving me."

Jessica's arms wrapped around her and hugged her close and said, "You are very welcome, sweetie. You can live with us and be save now. Is that OK?"

Sue started crying then, but Augie wasn't sure if it was relief of being safe or fear of losing her parents, probably both, but Sue wept out a loud, "OK."

This latest episode with the demons and saving another Alpha had really got her to thinking. Augie said, "Have you noticed that the Alphas have saved more Alphas than the Olympian gods, and we have done that by being on the ground among the people, well you have," pointing to Jessica? "I'm thinking the Alpha spirits are somehow sending us where we need to be to protect other Alphas. Think about it. What are the odds of being exactly where we needed to be to save this little girl? I also think the gods are still living in the third century and don't have a clue how the world works today. They have lived isolated there in Mount Olympus for centuries. I know they are trying to help, but if we wait on them, we will lose far too many Alphas. We need to support the actions of the Olympian gods, but we need to take action on the ground as well. What do you guys think?"

The all chimed in more or less together, agreeing.

Jessica said, "What do you have in mind, Augie?"

Augie continued, "Well, for one thing, we need to find out who is controlling the Omegas and from where. It would be helpful to know about the enemy. We can't do it. In truth, we don't have to do it. It's probably already being done, I'm thinking by the FBI. They don't know about the auras, but certainly there have been plenty of mutilation killings other than the ones we have killed, and they will have a team working on it, probably looking for us. I'm thinking we need to find someone we can work with there."

"Oh, by the way, if any of you have a cell phone, toss them out the window, now. The FBI has probably identified some of us, maybe even all, and they will be able to track us through our cell phones." Only Sue had a cell phone, which she handed to Jessica.

They were traveling through the back country headed south toward Muskogee. They passed through Wagoner and found an electronic store, where Augie purchased several untraceable pre-paid cell phones. She then found an isolated area to hide, while she began her work.

Her first call was to her attorney. Her wealth and his compensation ensured he would be willing to do whatever she wanted done, and her instructions to him was to find out who at the FBI was in charge of the mutilation killings.

59

# Chapter 4
# FBI

Jack Ward had had a long and lustrous career with the FBI. He had served the bureau in numerous capacities, one being assistant director of the FBI. He was now serving out his remaining time to retirement as a senior instructor at the FBI Academy at Quantico, Virginia. He was alone now, his wife having died three years ago. All his children had families of their own now and spread all over the country. Being alone, he had no idea what he would do when retirement finally came, and really wasn't looking forward to it.

The excitement came three day ago when he was pulled out of his class to talk to the Director of the FBI. "Yes, sir," he said, "How may I be of assistance?"

"Well, Jack," said the director, "I don't know if you have heard. The government is trying to put a lid on it, but all hell is breaking loose all over the country. We are also getting reports from Europe, hell, everywhere. I just got off the phone with the Attorney General, and he wants my best man on it, and you are him. Sorry to pull you off your cushy job at Quantico, Jack, but I need you at headquarters in D.C to take over this project, now."

"For heaven's sake, director," Jack said, "What project?"

The director said, "Oh, sorry, Jack. I'm still a little flustered from the ass chewing the AG motivated me with. It's like that damn movie that came out years ago, "Highlander" where people go around chopping off heads, but this is on a much bigger scale. Jack, some of those getting their heads chopped off are women, children and old people. You just need to get your butt to D.C. and quickly. I'm putting all resources of the FBI at your disposal. Hurry, Jack."

By the time he reached D.C. the place looked like a beehive, and all the department heads converged on him as he entered. They knew better than that; they must really be flustered. All he could do was call a department head briefing so he could find out just what was going on.

Over the last two day there had been fifty-two brutal mutilation deaths, five had been children, five had been elderly, and the rest had been, mostly men but also a few women. The deaths seemingly had no common ties to each other, but they continued to occur all over the world. They hadn't even been able to come up with any theories that made sense. They still had a lot of work to do.

Two days later they still hadn't made a connection. That's when he got the call.

"Are you Jack Ward, Special Agent in charge of the mutilation murders for the FBI?"

Jack said, "Yes, I understand that you have information concerning these murders?"

"Yes, I do. I know all about them. I know who they are and why they are happening. I will tell you everything, but I also need your help."

Jack said, "To Whom am I speaking?"

"Just call me Augie. Of course that is not my real name. If you want the answers you seek and are willing to help me, come outside and down Pennsylvania Avenue NW to Pershing Park. Bring a newspaper and place it on your head, and I will contact you."

***

Apollo announced to Zeus and the assembly that Augie and the warriors were ready to come back, and Zeus began the process. He noticed that the warriors had again hid the van for possible future use. He laughed, thinking, if it keeps them happy. Soon they will find a better way to travel.

Zeus was shocked at the new apparel and appearance of Heracles. It had been ages since he had seen Heracles and had forgotten just how intimidating he truly was/is, which was accented by his new dress. Heracles stood 6' 3" at, he estimated, around 275 lbs. and definitely was/is an extremely well built man in his physical prime...tall, dark, hugely muscled, and now also clad in black leather and spikes. His weapon of choice was a huge double-bladed battle-axe. Although massively muscled, which drew your attention, what any observer focused on were his wild eyes. The look radiated his barely controlled, internal rage, like a simmering volcano threatening to erupt at any moment. This man, his son, was dangerous, but he apparently smoothly interfaced with the others. From observation of battle in the mist, the team worked well together.

Apparently, Asteria's spirit hadn't recalled that Heracles had killed her in battle in their ancient lives. Maybe in time this memory could surface, but by then, hopefully, they would have a new bond to keep them working together. Initially, Zeus had thought to keep them apart, but Heracles' rage against the Omega seemed far stronger as a

62

motivation, and if Asteria remembered, she kept it to herself.

Zeus then turned to Athena, whose arms still held the small girl and asked in a fatherly tone, "Who do we have here, Athena?"

Athena said, "This is our newest recruit, Sue. I'm sure you saw the battle."

That last comment sounded somewhat like an accusation, but of course they had watched the warriors everywhere they went. Now he knew that they expected as much. He said, "Welcome, Sue. You are safe here."

He was truly surprised when Augie stepped forward and said, "We have a plan we would like to present to you and the Assembly." She then launched into the plan, including no small amount of instruction about the modern world and how it worked and could be used for their benefit.

He liked this lady. Her plan, and he had no doubt that it was her plan, was a daring plan, well thought out, and it made sense. She was, however, asking the Assembly to do things never done before, and he wasn't sure how the others would accept it. He said, "These requests are strange indeed, and it will require the entire Assembly to agree. How say you, gods?

Their eyes all followed the vote of the Assembly as it went around. All the votes were yes, so he announced, "We agree. You are in charge of this plan, and we will follow your instruction." After a pause he said, "For this plan, only!"

\*\*\*

Augie watched as a ruggedly handsome Jack Ward came out of FBI headquarters and walked

63

down the sidewalk toward the park, at least she thought it must be Jack Ward, since he carried a newspaper under his arm. He was a tall, lean man, maybe in his early sixties with short greying hair but still laced with plenty of black. He looked like an FBI agent, clean shaven and dressed in a dark blue suit with a red tie.

Another reason she knew it was Jack Ward: she also watched as agents followed him at a distance. There were also agents already positioned in the park, but she fully expected these precautions. Augie had fully expected them to attempt to capture her and interrogate her for what she knew under their terms, but that was not her plan.

Jack Ward walked into the park and looked around. He then placed the paper on his head and waited, but he didn't expect what happened next. His body began to shimmer, then he popped out of existence in full view and shock of his agents. They ran toward him, but he was no longer there. He was materializing within the mist on Mount Olympus.

Jack Ward stood frozen and panicked in the center of the Assembly of gods. Augie quickly stepped forward and said, "Relax, no harm will come to you. Sorry, Mr. Ward, for the dramatics, but it was necessary so you will believe the story we have to tell you. Without you experiencing and seeing with your own eyes what we have to tell you, there is no way you would believe. Now I dare say, you will believe. Are you OK, Mr. Ward?"

His eyes were wide, but he took in everything. At least he was no longer in danger of heart failure. Jack said, "Yes, I'm shook up and don't understand what is going on, but I'm certainly ready to listen."

Augie continued, "We need your help, and without us you will never understand what is happening with these mutilation killing. I will just give you some facts. Don't question them or ask questions. You are here, so you must believe. You are at Mount Olympus and these are the Olympian gods. That is all you need to know about them right now. What the world is experiencing now is a war of the descendants of a race of people known as the Titans. There are good ones and bad ones. We are the good ones, and you will learn this in time. The war will result in total genocide of one side or the other. What you need to know is that the bad side has flourished on Earth until now. Believe it or not, we fully suspect that they are well established in all governments on Earth. If you help us they may also come against you, so be prepared. We do have certain powers to wage the battle, but our bodies are easily killed, just like any human. The battle is not about the body. It is about the Titan spirit. It must be killed by decapitation of the occupied body. This war must be waged, and you need to know that if we fail, the bad side will plunge Earth into despicable evil, and the human race will no longer be the dominant race."

"If you remember back a few days to the sunspots that generated a bluish light for several days. That was a Titan energy beam designed to wake up the good side. That is when the killing began. We call ourselves Alphas. We were awakened to kill the Omegas and save Earth, but they were already awake and waiting for us. They are killing the Alphas as they awaken, except for a few of us that have managed to survive their attacks. They can see our auras and attack us. We can see their auras also. Unfortunately, humans can see neither aura. This is how we know who to fight, but the truth be known, so far we have only killed in self-defense."

"So you will believe, our friend Hermes here has created a pair of magical sunglasses, so you will be able to see the auras." She handed them to Mr. Ward. When he put them on she asked, "Do you see our auras?"

He looked around the room in amazement and said, "Well, I be dammed."

"Let's hope not, Mr. Ward, but when you see one of the Omegas you might think you are damned. Their auras are red and literally look like the demons they truly are. You will be able to see them with these glasses, but I suggest you tell no one. They are far more numerous and are everywhere, probably even in the FBI. If you are wondering if the glasses can be duplicated, the answer is, no. Hermes built them with magic just for you."

"Now, what we need from you. We don't know where the Omegas are headquartered. Now that you know the truth behind the killings, your team will be able to find them. They are not random; they are all controlled from somewhere. You must find them for us."

"We also need you to help us save the Alphas, and the only identifying feature is the golden auras. At this point, most don't even know who they are. They are confused. We need you to advertise that the sunspots can affect some people, making them

66

believe they glow. Tell them this condition can be treated and set up a call-in line for their calls."

"This is the tricky part. It won't take long for the Omegas to realize what you are doing and tap in. Once someone calls in to describe a golden aura, you must be quick to retrieve them or notify us, and we will go get them. As you have seen, we can travel fast. If you are successful in retrieving any of the Alphas, you must protect them, because the Omegas will stop at nothing to kill an Alpha."

"Will you help us, Mr. Ward? You will save lives, some of them children. Will you help us save Earth from becoming a living hell?"

He thought for a moment, looked around again, then nodded and said, "I am thinking there are no telephones here, wherever here is. How will I notify you?"

Beautiful Aphrodite spoke, "I will remain focused on you. All you have to do is think my name, Aphrodite, and I will hear you and your message."

***

Jack was bombarded by question when he materialized back in the park, and he didn't know how to answer them. He simply waved off the questions and returned to his office to ponder all he had learned. The one thing he knew for sure was it had not been a dream. His agents had seen him disappear and reappear. It was real, and it made perfect sense.

He quickly got on the internet and typed in "Olympian gods." He then clicked on Wikipedia, "Twelve Olympians", then on "Aphrodite". There was a picture of a statue of Aphrodite. In the statue she was stunningly beautiful, but not nearly as beautiful as he remembered seeing her in person. Just think her name? How could he do anything but? She had dressed simply, wrapping her gorgeous body with a white wrap and thankfully not all of that body. The only other adornment had been a blue flower garland wrapping the top of her head, but then her beauty needed no adornment.

He read that Aphrodite was the daughter of Zeus, the supreme god of the Olympians. He had no doubt that Zeus was the imposing figure at the main thorn, though he never heard his name.

Next he clicked on Hermes, the other name he heard. He was also described as a son of Zeus and was described as wearing winged sandals and hat, which indeed he remembered seeing. It also mentioned that Hermes also carried a magic wand, which also fit the making of the glasses.

He clicked on down the list, but couldn't put names to those he had seen. Jack was fairly positive he recognize Apollo, because the description commented about Apollo being beardless and athletic, and he remembered him as so. He also thought he placed Artemis, Apollo's twin sister, by her similar look. Ares was also easy to identify by his helmet, shield and spear listed in his description.

Oh well, he didn't have time to figure it all out right now, and he was sure it would all become clear in time. Jack didn't know how, but the one thing he was sure of was that he apparently had actually met the Olympian gods. He was thinking, It was all believable. While he was considering these facts, he was toying with the glasses. If he believed, then the magical glasses must also be true.

He slipped them on and left his office to walk the halls.

As he left his office his second in command fell in beside him. He was obviously anxious to find out what the hell was going on. Jack surveyed the beehive of activity in the room to see if there were any of the so called Omega, but he saw nothing. Damn, could this be an elaborate hoax? If it was, it was a good one. He kept walking down the halls, looking, but he was starting to feel very silly, when he turned a corner and found himself staring directly into the eyes of a demon. He froze and clamped down on his expressions, providing no outward sign of the recognition. He was suddenly thankful for his experience and training that allowed him to freeze his expressions. The demon continued to walk past him and down the hall. Jack turned to his second and asked, "Who was that we just met?"

His second said, "I'm not sure, since we have so many new agents assigned to this project. Why do you ask?"

"This is a very sensitive project. I may ask you to transfer or reassign certain agents at my whim. Please do so, starting with that one. I don't want him involved directly in this project."

"Yes, sir, I will see to it immediately," said his second.

"Don't make it obvious. Assign him to do something not associated directly with the senior agents, and get him out of this office."

Jack found two other demons at headquarters, and one was an assistant director, but neither were involved directly with his project. He had his second assign agents to research their background, watch them and report back.

The next assignment he gave to his second was the news release about the sunspots causing some mental disorientation, and giving out an information number for those affected. The symptom to watch for was a delusional glow. If they experience this symptom, call the treatment line immediately.

He knew he would have to come up with a good excuse for his director and second, but he would cross that bridge when he came to it. The easier task was the background follow-up of the dead. He had the team concentrate on the men. He wanted to know everything about them ... find a connecting tie, even if they had to trace the companies they worked for all the way back to the investors. This is something the FBI excelled in, and it would only be a matter of time now before he knew what to look for.

# Chapter 5
# The Trap

Mojo was livid with the reports coming in. He had lost many agents at the hands of the Alphas. They were learning how to survive far too quickly. Some of his Omega spirits hadn't been killed outright and were absorbed into other Omega hosts gathered for this purpose. These reports would be far more informative, so he had them report to him. He wanted to hear them firsthand.

He listened to the reports from the first four that had been killed in Charlotte, North Carolina at the same time and was amazed that they had all been killed by a single individual ... a small woman. Even though she had used a gun at close range, it didn't figure that she could have shot them all without at least one of his soldiers getting to her. Did she have powers already? She must have used time alteration. Damn that bastard, Zeus for awakening her powers.

The next soldier Mojo interviewed had been a spotter for two demons assigned to kill an elderly Alpha in Nashville, Tennessee. The older woman had been identified via a modified NSA satellite and reported by his agents imbedded there. Mojo had immediately dispatched agents to kill her, and it should have been an easy kill. The woman had been saved at the last minute by another young Alpha. The soldier's description sounded very much like the same Alpha in Charlotte. The cities weren't that far apart, so it was possible. What disturbed him most was the description of the small lady's golden aura, an owl. Could this be a descendant of Athena? An owl was her mascot. If so, she must be killed at once before she became fully awake. Athena had been very powerful.

There were no surviving Omegas from the next engagement, and five more soldiers perished in St. Louis. Field agents on the ground had been tracking a black lady Alpha into an alley, but the hosts and spirits were all killed, beheaded. The spotter he interviewed had seen a black van speeding off, which seemed to imply several Alphas together. The timing was about right; the Charlotte Alpha could have made it to St. Louis traveling in a black van. So, she was traveling west. He took a quick look at a map and immediately dispatched soldiers, many of them to Tulsa, Oklahoma and Oklahoma City. This group must be destroyed before they could gather more Alphas and grow in power.

Next he talked to the human recipients of the two Omegas from California. The soldiers had been killed, but the spirits survived. The host bodies had been attacked by a huge muscular Alpha man in San Diego. The Alpha ran, but ten of his soldiers gave chase directed by satellite tracking from one of his agents at the National Security Agency (NSA).

What Mojo saw next on the NSA tapes transferred to him boiled his rage. As he watched the ten soldiers corner the male Alpha in an alley, three additional Alphas materialized beside the male Alpha. Together the four Alphas charged his soldiers. What he previously suspected about the Alphas being able to alter time proved correct. His soldiers moved in slow motion, while the Alphas sped through them and sent their heads flying.

He knew then for sure that his brother, Zeus had saved them and was leading and augmenting them. Damn him! Zeus was beginning to foul up his plans for Earth. He would fail, and he would pay.

***

Jessica was tired and bored of sitting around. She was, however, very pleased to have company now, and knew she was lucky to still be alive. It was like she had lived an entire life full of excitement in the few days of being an Alpha.

Azlana was likable and very competent as a warrior, and they had become good friends. I guess saving someone makes you appear friendly, certainly Azlana trusted both Jessica and Augie, and the feeling was mutual.

Heracles was unbelievable. He was massive and his damned arms were almost as big as her waist, but he was always full of seething rage, just barely controlled. As a result he remained quiet and reserved and didn't communicate much. But, he was certainly a welcome member of the team.

Augie was turning into the mother hen of the team, and Jessica liked her, a lot. She was a natural leader. During their conversations Jessica discovered that Augie was not just wealthy from marriage, but had helped built a large computer company, which she recently sold. Augie was just getting used to her retirement and learning to walk everywhere. That's how the Omega spotted her and how Jessica found her, seemingly by accident. Still, she felt that it was not really an accident and some

73

power directed her to that exact place and at the right time.

Sue was a little sweetheart, so young and open. Being taken from her parents had her more than a little frightened, though. Jessica had immediately taken her under her wing and care and welcomed by both. Sue needed to be taken care of, though, and Jessica had decided Sue would live with her.

The quarters they were given to live in were all exactly the same, nothing fancy. The basics were provided: bed, chair, table, something resembling a bathroom, and food was delivered, but nothing more. Well, there was something else in each unit, a smaller version of the dais in the thorn room. She had no idea why, since it didn't appear to be active. These identical living area were widely circled around the central thorn room, but she noticed that few were occupied, only the Alphas.

Within this circled area were trees, gardens and a large swimming pool, or maybe a common bath. Little else was there, and it all felt quiet and tranquil.

When they were all gathered earlier, visiting and comparing notes, they all complained about having nothing in the form of entertainment. There were no TVs, radios, or electronics of any kind. Even the lighting seemed to just be there, and come to think of it, there was no day or night. It was always bright, but she saw no sun. There also was no wind, and the temperature seems always perfect.

Azlana even said, "These gods don't seem to do anything except sit on their thorns, stare into the mist, and think about sex. I see the way Zeus and the others keep staring at Jessica and I, and if I were

you, Heracles, I sure wouldn't go over there alone."
At that remark, everyone laughed, but it was true;
the hungry looks were hard to miss.

The Alphas could easily become bored living
here. Maybe they would have to go shopping more
often, maybe even live down there. Puzzling over
her own statement, she wondered if Mount
Olympus was up? She saw nothing outside of
Mount Olympus, just lazy white clouds. Hell, it
might even be in a different dimension or something
else just as bizarre.

Augie came in through her quarter's archway
opening, since there were no doors to shut. Augie
was checking on Sue, the mother hen. As they were
chatting, Augie's eyes appeared to look inward, and
she went silent. When her eyes refocused she said,
"Aphrodite just informed me that Mr. Ward has
located another Alpha, and they want us to join
them in the Assembly chamber."

Augie called the others and they left
immediately for the chamber. As they entered the
chamber they could see the vision in the mist focus
and zoom in on a street then expanded to only a
house.

Aphrodite said, "According to Mr. Ward, a lady
called in from this address in Fultondale, Alabama,
a suburb of Birmingham. The woman said she saw
a golden glow in the mirror and thought she was
going crazy until she heard on the news about the
sunspot reaction and called in. She wants the
treatment, and we are sending you to her.

Zeus said, "We are ready. Enter the mist."

Before entering, Jessica looked to Augie and
said, "Can you stay here and look after Sue?"

Before Augie could answer, Hestia, Zeus' sister said, "Augie needs to go with you for communication. I will look after Sue." Hestia then smiled at Sue and took her hand and walked off toward the gardens.

***

Karrie Sparks heard the news report about the recent sunspots triggering a form of dementia in some people. It was reported that this form of dementia made the brain appear to see colored auras. They said not to worry that it could be treated. They gave the 800 number to call for treatment. Karrie took a deep a breath of relief, because she thought she was having some sort of mental breakdown. Not only was she seeing a golden aura, but she was remembering an ancient life. None of it made sense to her.

The first time she saw the golden glow, it scared her half to death. It wasn't just the glow; it was the shape it took. It appeared to form into the shape of two large snakes, pythons size, but with fangs. The snakes were huge and wrapped around her body to hover and sway back and forth over her head. Even in the bright golden glow the eyes shown an even brighter red and very scary.

She had just finished a shower when she discovered the glowing shakes, and she screamed and quickly wrapped her robe around her and ran into the living room of their home. Her parents were on the couch and she quickly jumped between them, startling them. After a few seconds she realized they didn't see the snakes. With that realization, she took to simply hiding in her room

76

and refused to go to school. Something was very wrong, and she didn't know what.

Her parents were very concerned that she didn't want to go to school, because she had just made the cheerleading squad at Fultondale High School, and she had been excited about that. It was quite a feat for a Sophomore. Although concerned for their only child, her parents let her have her space to work out whatever it was that was bothering her.

Karrie finally came bursting out of her room and told them what had been bothering her. Her parents called the number immediately, anxious to get her the treatment they mentioned. They were told just to wait at home and a team of doctors would come there and treat Karrie, and that's just what they did.

Karrie didn't see the vans get there, but she heard the doorbell ring and her parents let them inside. When she came out she screamed at the horrific red demon glows that met her. That's when they pulled out swords and killed her parents right in front of her. One was about to kill her, when the others stopped him, saying we might need her to draw the others in. She didn't hear anything else, because they knocked her out cold. Several time she woke up just to be beaten again. After a while she stopped trying to wake up.

*\*\**

Jessica led her team into the mist for transport and materialized precisely on the front porch of the target home. She knocked on the door and after a few seconds the curtain pulled back slightly on the window, and, luckily for them, she glimpsed a slight glow of red. She screamed, "It's a trap! Run!"

77

They sped into the front yard as the porch exploded with shrapnel. It was a brilliant plan designed not to kill outright but to incapacitate them so the demons could kill them in the proper way. Their plan almost worked. They didn't have time to celebrate, however, as the red demons burst out the door and from around both sides of the house. There must have been thirty Omaga demons converging on her group of Alphas. They were on them so fast they didn't have time to mount a proper defense, so they circled around Augie, while she concentrated hard and raised her arms high in the air.

Everything changed then. The demons were close, but they appeared to almost stop in their tracks. Augie's power over time was growing ... thankfully. The demons continued to move but very slowly now. Heracles laughed a crazy laugh then bellowed his rage and attacked the demons. They couldn't move out of his way, and he went through them like he was cutting wheat. She and Azlana gave Heracles room for him to make his full swings, while they began working their way around the circle of demons.

As she was fighting, well little fighting, just killing. Jessica said, "Augie, you got that time adjustment trick down good now; much better than I. Thanks. You saved us." It was easy slaughter, but they were demons, and they were hell bent on murdering them.

Once they completed killing the auras, she went inside to look around. It had been an elaborate trick to trap them, but she wasn't sure if it was totally fabricated, or if it was based upon truth about an

Alpha in fact being here. Jessica canvased the house and in the last bedroom found a weak glowing Alpha knocked unconscious. There were two other older humans that must have been her parents, but they were dead. They hadn't been mutilated, indicating that the humans were probably normal humans. She heard sirens in the distance, so she quickly helped the weak Alpha out of the house, where Heracles, strangely staring at the unconscious girl, then quickly picked the dazed Alpha up in his arms and carried her back to join the group.

Augie quickly asked Aphrodite to transport them back, and they watched the greatly excited neighbors and police disappear, to be replaced by Zeus and the Assembly.

***

Zeus and the Assembly watched the battle in the mist. It frightened and angered him how the Omega had set the trap. The Omegas had undeniably used the FBI agent, whether the agent knew or not, but Augie's plan did, however, function to locate another Alpha. Unfortunately, the Omegas would and did instantly identify the news reports for what they were, an effort to locate Alphas, and deployed to intercept and use the information coming in to their advantage. His anger surged with the realization that he and the Assembly and his warriors had been tricked and almost defeated. Damn his brother, Hades!

His anger was offset by his pleasure, however, with the instant growth of Augie's power over time control. It was not fully developed, but she had grown drastically with the absolute need to survive.

Augie also brought with her the knowledge of how the modern world worked. He had no interest in their narrow and limited view of life, but this knowledge seemed necessary now to find more Alphas and fight the obviously knowledgeable Omegas. Augie might prove invaluable in this role. Initially he thought this elderly woman would be useless, but she was proving to be a valuable addition to the warrior team.

He focused his thoughts as the team's molecules reconstructed within the mist. They had succeeded, barely, in killing the demons and saving another Alpha. This raven haired Alpha was also petite and young, maybe sixteen years old, a child. Heracles still carried the girl effortlessly in his arms and showed no inclination to put her down, but she was welcome. She was somewhat awake now but had her arms wrapped tightly around Heracles' thick neck. Zeus thought she was still probably in shock from the ordeal, but she turned to him and stared into his eyes. In that instant Zeus recognized her Titan Spirit. This was another beautiful, daughter, beauty so legendary that wars had been fought over her.

Aphrodite also knew her ancient friend and said, "It's Helen, Helen of Troy. Do you know me, Helen?"

The girl shook her head and said, "No. My name is Karrie."

Zeus said with some authority and no small amount of impatience, "No, you are Helen! You are now a Dark Angel. The other Angels will explain everything to you when you calm down some."

Augie stepped forward and said, "We were tricked today. I need to be able to communicate better with Jack Ward." She also spoke with authority and pent up aggravation.

"Well, do so!" Zeus barked.

Augie barked back, "I don't see any damn telephones! How in the hell do you propose I communicate with him?"

Zeus' anger was immediate and abundantly apparent to the other gods, who seemed to recoil into their individual thrones. He didn't allow others to talk to him with such little respect. He demanded respect. Many have tried through the centuries, but none succeeded. But, he held his temper, thinking. Augie is an Alpha, but still mostly human. Her spirit will fully awake, but it would take a while. She didn't yet understand who they were and who she herself was.

He calmed and said, "All of you listen to what I have to tell you. You will remember in time for yourself and eventually not have to show your ignorance and limitations, but there are things you need to understand now in order to survive. We will speak of this only this once and never again in the open. Understood?"

"We here are gods and have powers, and you are gods, at least you have a god inside you. Our original race was mostly energy, mind. We have existed for eons, but not always in these forms. Once we were pure energy, but we created forms to experience emotions and pleasure, something we did not have in the pure form. Now we are committed to our forms and can't return."

"Our entire race lives through our daises; it is an extension of us, our power. It takes our minds anywhere, any place, any time we wish to be, and through the dais we have the ability to manipulate matter. What you need to understand is, if you want a damned telephone or anything else, you can make one in your own dais in your quarters, but that is an extremely simple explanation, too simple. We create whatever technology we need, but what happens is far more complex than simple technology. It is a physical reality we make happen, which you humans call magic, because humans don't understand it and can't explain it. Earth's technology is far too limited and simple. In truth we simply make it work for us when we desire to. Now, unfortunately, we haven't lived in the world in centuries, and we don't know what technology is available to utilize. Augie, that is where you can be a valuable asset. You want a phone? Go learn how to make one and make it work. We can't make you a phone, because we don't even know what a phone is or what it does."

"As a result of human influence over centuries, you Alphas aren't bound to your dais like we are, but your Alpha spirit can work through a dais, with limitations."

"I need others of the Assembly to help indoctrinate the Dark Angles, also. They have a lot to learn, and if they hadn't grown and expanded their abilities today, they would be dead and this war already lost. I don't need to remind you that if the Dark Angels die, we will soon follow."

Maybe he revealed too much, but he was in charge and felt that they needed to know. As he

82

surveyed the other gods for their approval, he saw no menacing reactions, even from his brother, Poseidon, who has never been slow to criticize when he needed it.

***

Augie had a new sense of reality dawning. Zeus had handed her some control over herself and the other Angels, at least it was as close as it was going to get. Zeus had apparently broken some unspoken Olympian law by revealing these secrets to them, but he had done so to help them. In doing so, he had spoken of unspeakable things, deep secrets. Unfortunately, the things of which he spoke were so cryptic it was difficult to understand the meaning of the secrets. It would take time to sort it all out, so the Angels dismissed themselves and returned to their quarters.

Of course no one went to their quarters; they all came to hers, including Sue, who had quickly rejoined Jessica. But, the first one to speak was Karrie. Still perched in Heracles' arms, she said, "What in the blazes were those people in there? What the hell is a 'Dark Angel'? Where are we? Who the hell were those red glowing bastards that killed my parents? Why do we all glow gold? Who are you by the way?" She would have continued rattling off questions like bullets from an automatic weapon had it not been for the fact that the whole group burst out laughing at her verbal bombardment. Although serious, especially with the murder of her parents, her explosion of fast-paced questions allowed no time for responses. It struck everyone as humorous. Karrie started to get offended, but realized what she had done and

83

eventually joined in the laughter. The fact that Karrie was still cradled in Heracles' arms added to the humor.

Augie said, "Heracles, geez, put her down; she has legs. Karrie, we will try to answer all your question." All the Angels began answering her questions in detail, offering information and individual perspectives. Karrie also began a detailed description of her experience.

After the sunspot activity, Karrie observed her golden glow, but she believed her mind was playing tricks on her or becoming deranged. For days she simply hid, refusing to go to school. Her parents were concerned, but she didn't share her worries with them until she heard the news report about the sunspots triggering mental responses in some people. The main symptom of this ailment was a belief of a body glow. Karrie leaped upon this revelation and potential solution. Finally, she told her parents, and since this information was on the news, her parents reluctantly believed her problem was real and called the "Information Hot Line". They were told to wait there and a team would be dispatched to come and treat her.

After five or so hours of waiting, a van, several vans actually, pulled up. Karrie did not see the demon auras until the first group came inside. She screamed, and the red demons killed her parents when they tried to protect her. She thought they were going to kill her, but they tied her up instead. They had commented among themselves that she might be needed alive to lure the others in. "Obviously, you guys are the others they referred to," Karrie said.

84

While the discussion was going on, Augie was watching Karrie. She hadn't really noticed how truly beautiful she was. Sure, she and everyone else noticed that she was pretty, but for the first time she took a really good look. She had long, silky, raven black hair that accented intense ocean blue eyes. It was an interesting and mesmerizing combination. She was slightly larger than Jessica but still quite petite. Obviously, Heracles found her beautiful, but she suspected he found her beautiful in other ways also.

Augie noticed that Heracles never took his eyes off Karrie and paid rapt attention to everything she said. She also noticed that Heracles was now the calmest she had ever seen him. If for this reason alone, Karrie was already contributing to the team. More amazing, Karrie never left his side, and most of the time she touched him in some casual way, mostly unnoticed by the others. There was apparently some deeper connection here, possibly associated with the spirits or some past life. Damn, now she was talking cryptic and had no idea what she meant, but she took notice.

Something Karrie said caught her attention, and Augie began mulling over some of the facts as Karrie had described them, and something didn't make sense. The Dark Angels had left almost immediately upon notification to retrieve Karrie, but Karrie said they waited over five hours for the demons to show up. Either Mr. Ward lied about the timing or someone lied to him. She really hoped she could trust him, because they needed help, and they didn't have a lot of options. She needed to communicate with him, and like Zeus had said, "Just Do it. Create a phone and make it work."

She ran everyone out so she could concentrate on making a phone, but first she must figure out how to turn the dais on. There wouldn't be any switches. It would have to be mental control by the Titan spirit, which evidently she had. Somehow she had to bring forward her spirit and let her mind mingle with it. But how?

From just inside her quarters Poseidon spoke, startling her, "Don't think about it, just let it happen. Work backwards. As humans might say, reverse engineer." Then, as quickly as he came, he turned and left. These Titans didn't seem to have much motivation or drive, something else to wonder about.

Work backwards? Okay. Her mind sought Mr. Ward. She relaxed and let her mind stream from her ... out...toward Mr. Ward. Augie was vaguely aware of the mist forming, but her consciousness flowed into the mist and out. Her mind thought ... Mr. Ward, and her whole point of reference shot out toward him. After the initial flush of vertigo, she just let her mind continue its journey. She didn't know where he was, but the mist knew and took her mind there. Soon she was flowing into a building and floating in the air above his desk. Augie thought cell-phone and Jack's phone began to outline itself in his pocket. Why did she think that? She knew he had a cell-phone. What she needed was a cell-phone for herself and his number. The mist began to sparkle and concentrate, forming and slowly solidifying a cell-phone to hover in the mist before her. She tentatively reached out and took it.

When she touched her phone, Jack's cell-phone began to ring. She quickly placed her new phone to her ear, and she heard the call ringing then she heard, "Jack Ward."

Augie forgot the dais and the magic when she heard his voice. She also remembered her anger and yelled, "Mr. Ward! You almost got us killed, you bastard!"

"Is that you, Augie?" he said.

"Hell yes, it's me! Why did you wait five hours to let us know you found an Alpha? They were waiting on us when we arrived, and we had to fight our way out!" she screamed.

Mr. Ward responded, "I notified my contact immediately as soon as I was informed. There was no five hour delay! Wait. Let me check on something. Can I call you back at this number?"

"Yeah. I'll wait for your call." She had no idea if she even had a number, but she intended to watch him anyway.

# Chapter 6
# Collaboration

Jack Ward was shocked with the call and especially Augie's hostility. He had notified Aphrodite immediately. He had thought her name, even said it out loud to be sure, then delivered the address where the call had come in from. Obviously, they had gotten the message if they had gone there. Five hours delay? A trap? Something was definitely wrong, and it had to be on his end.

He grabbed his special sunglasses and bounded out of his office, only to almost run over his second. Jack grabbed him by the shoulders and said, "Where did you set up the special call in team? Never mind. Take me there, now!"

Jack followed his frazzled assistant to the elevators, down two levels, around the corner and down the hall. His assistant pointed to a large open office area. Jack stopped him with a hand on his shoulders outside the glass wall. Through his glasses he immediately saw three of the damned red demons working there. Jack grabbed his assistant then and pushed him on down the hall with him and said, "Come with me. We are going to see the director, but first I want a witness."

Jack's main concern was to keep his ability to identify the demons a secret. So, he instructed his assistant carefully and put the glasses on him, while they walked back by the office. His assistant stiffened, but he pulled him along down the hall before any of the demons could notice any reaction.

He marched into the office of the Director of the FBI with his assistant in tow and demanded to see the director immediately. After a quick intercom call, the administrative assistant sent them in. Jack had kept his glasses on trying to identify other demons, but he had not seen any more. That stood to reason; the demons were concentrating on the threat of the Alphas at all cost, and from what Augie had said it had almost worked. It was his fault; he should have anticipated this.

Jack remained anxious until he personally saw the director and the absence of a red aura. As soon as they were seated Jack launched into his spiel, "Director, I am in well over my head on this project and don't have the authority necessary to deal with it. I'm afraid it will require your direct involvement. You may even want to get others involved outside of the Bureau, but that's your call, obviously."

"Is this about the mutilation murders?" asked the director.

"Yes, Sir, but that's not what it's about. This is a war, a war among aliens. Maybe I should just tell you the story as I have experienced it to date, but I suggest that you activate your office security first."

Director Setliff was a medium built man in his early sixties, balding, and his shoulders were slightly bowed from years of desk work, but after switching on the security he set up high in his chair in rapt attention and said, "From the seriousness of your expression I will assume this is no joke and by aliens, you don't mean French or Mexican immigrant?"

"No, Sir, I'm talking ET, and I couldn't be more serious," said Jack.

"Very well, let's hear the story," said the director.

Jack told him everything and in great detail right up to the involvement a few moments ago with the demons now controlling the "Hot Line." The director did not interrupt, even though he was visibly upset with the situation.

Director Setliff looked at Jack's assistant and said, "And you saw these demons, too?"

His assistant, Jim Taylor, had been totally silent up to this point, partly because most of what he was hearing was new information to him, and partly because he was obviously intimidated by the director, but he managed to nod and say, "Yes, Sir, and they are damn scary...Sir."

The director thought for a moment and said, "If I put those glasses on, I'll be able to see them, too?"

"Yes, Sir."

The director's forehead wrinkled in thought, made up his mind and picked up the phone. After a moment he spoke into the phone, "This is Director Setliff. I want this entire facility in full lockdown, NOW! Consider it a full terrorist alert with full activation of all weapons. No one leaves or enters. Cut all communication and activate the jammers to disable all wireless communications. I want a fully armed security team to meet me outside my office in ten minutes. Am I understood?" The security breech alarms came on immediately. The Director then looked at Jack and said, "We don't want them getting any word out, and we want to catch them all. Now let's go take back control of the 'Hot Line' then gather up these demons, lock them up and see what we can learn from them."

By the time they walked out of the director's office nine minutes later a ten-man fully armed security team stood to attention. Director Setliff waved them to follow, as he briskly marched down the hall, slipping on the sunglasses.

Before they even reached the elevators, the director stopped in his tracks, staring. He took the glasses off and handed them to him and said, "Is that what they look like?"

When he slipped them on he immediately saw the angry red glow and outline of a repulsive demon coming from a man that just exited the elevator. More shocking was the fact that the man housing the demon was an assistant director to Director Setliff. The assistant director rushed toward Director Setliff and said, "Sir, what's going on?"

"What's going on is that you are under arrest for terrorism! Security, secure this man in detention, and don't allow him to communicate with anyone." barked the director. They moved on and didn't look back, even at the sounds of a scuffle behind them.

The rules of a lockdown requires everyone to return to their assigned workplace or office, so as they reached the large office of the "Hot Line" there were four demons standing inside. The director led the group inside and began pointing to each of the four and said, "Security, take these gentlemen into custody and put them in the detention facility with the other. They are to be charged with terrorist activity. Now, Mr. Taylor, dig into this department and see how much damage they have done. Oh, they are scary, aren't they?"

"Okay, Jack, let's go through this whole damned building and clean them out, but maybe we should start with our internal security and police, since they have weapons."

***

Augie followed Mr. Ward in the mist of her dais through the whole process, and she no longer doubted him. She also saw what had happened. The Omegas had taken over the call center, which she noticed right away. Damn them. This is how they had set up the trap, but what pissed her off more was thinking about how many Alphas they might have intercepted and killed. Jim Taylor would soon be able to figure it all out.

She continued to let her mind hover over Mr. Ward and the director as they continued through the complex. They discovered no other demons, but maintained the communication black out. From what she gathered they were trying to figure out how to purge the FBI of all the demons. There biggest concern was what they would tell the other FBI agencies, especially Quantico, when they reactivated the communications. They had to use a believable cover story, and the director intended to use terrorism for this cover. He mentioned that they could hold the demons at Gitmo, and no one would know. But, they had to know who to trust and if they were talking to demons. They had to find and identify them, and it would be hard to do with only one pair of glasses.

Even though they maintained the communication black out, she thought her phone would still work, since her magic made hers and probably made his work to receive her calls. Magic was good, she thought. Her need to talk to Mr. Ward made his phone ring. Surprised, he answered, "Mr. Ward."

"Jack." She felt she could trust him now, like a friend. He had proven himself. "You have done well. I have followed your activities, and I want to help," she said.

"As you know, I am only days old myself as an Alpha, but I am learning fast. I need you to check on something for me. Do you have cameras in the detention area where the demons are kept?"

"Yes," Jack said.

"I need to know if the auras show up on camera," she said, "I need you to check."

"Alright. Hold on."

As he placed his phone on the nearest security console, he told the director who he was talking to and what I asked him to do. The director seemed anxious but nodded assent. She could tell immediately when Jack keyed in the security cameras that the auras didn't pass through, but she waited for Jack to confirm this knowledge. When he came back reporting to the negative, Augie said, "Too bad. OK, tell me who you are concerned about at Quantico and I will check them out. I can do it quickly." Jack quickly relayed the message to the director.

Jack said, "The director is mostly concerned with the director there, Mr. Mosley."

"OK, stay on the line," she said. Augie let her mind go and watched the perspective as it seemed her mind raced toward Quantico and homed in to

93

hover over Mr. Mosley in his office. He was a large imposing black man in his late forties. He was obviously distraught with the situation at FBI Headquarters, but he had no demon aura. "He is clear of an aura," she said, "If you like, I can follow him through the complex and point out any demons."

"Thank you for the good news. The director will be happy to hear it. As for your offer, we will have to wait. There is more pressing need. My assistant has identified three other Alphas that called in. The demons had been holding notification of them, evidently to give time to dispatch other demons to those locations."

Augie quickly jotted down the three locations and time of the calls and gave a hasty good-bye. On her way out of her quarters she gave out a piercing whistle and yelled, "Dark Angles, we're up!" She didn't know how, but Zeus and the assembly were ready for them when they came in. She handed the note with the addresses to Aphrodite, but she waved off the effort. Truth be known, Aphrodite or one of the other gods had probably been tuned in to her conversation in one form or another.

As they entered the mist, Zeus said, "We are too late on the first address, the Alpha is already dead. The second address is only two hours old, so it is a race." Augie thought, Oh, crap, as they began to shimmer in the mist.

*** 

Ralph Henderson was old, and some days he felt even older. He was seventy-five years old, still, his overall health was good. Sometimes this was depressing, because he was alone, and dying didn't seem so bad. His wife of forty years died almost two years ago, and their only son had been killed in a car accident years earlier. To add to the loneliness, he had always been around kids, having taught in the Scottsdale Unified School District in Arizona for forty years. Unfortunately, he had retired from teaching the year before his wife died. Now he didn't have his wife or the kids, some retirement.

He had loved teaching the young minds; they soaked in knowledge like sponges. His last teaching position was at Chaparral High School, where he taught history and the sciences, and he really missed it. He liked the interface with the kids and felt that he was doing some good. Now he spent his time keeping the best kept lawn and garden in his neighborhood, keeping the birds fed, an occasionally a few rounds of golf, and anything that kept him out in the sun and off the couch.

His routine of make work stopped four days ago with the appearance of the golden aura. It didn't frighten him; it was actually comforting. He had thought about getting a cat for company, but this cat was in the form of an aura that encompassed his entire body, and in truth it was a little much. This one looked like the roaring lion on an MGM move header. He just admired it, but it did make him feel a little self-conscious about going outside. He really didn't know if it was in his mind or if others might be able to see it, so he stayed inside.

Things began to make a little more sense when he heard the reports about sunspots causing a form of dementia. He supposed that was possible. Surely, that is what this was, but they said there was a treatment. So, he call the "Hot Line". They took his information and address and suggested that he just stay inside and wait for the treatment team to come. So, that's what he did ... wait.

***

George Brawley was a spoiled kid, mainly because his father was a wealthy real estate mogul in Orlando, Florida, but he knew he was spoiled and was not under any delusion. He was an only child and raised in money. He really never had a chance ... too much money, too much time on his hand, and no supervision. But, somewhere along the line he developed a strong fascination and love of the ocean, and spent much of his time, sailing, SCUBA diving, water skiing or anything else to do with the water. One of his favorite places in the world was the Miami Seaquarium and visited there often. This unexplained love of the sea led to a strong desire to be an oceanographer, which led him to the University of Miami and the Rosenstiel School of Marine and Atmospheric Science. This choice of colleges was not so surprising, since it was adjacent to the Miami Seaquarium.

His father bought him a condo in Coral Gables, just across the Rickenbacker Causeway from his school on Virginia Key. This is where he was when the awakening came. The sickness had lasted several days, but today he awoke knowing who he was after years of sensing it. Even as a young boy he knew he was somehow special, not in the privileged sense but in a different way. He felt it but didn't understand it. It was like it was in his blood. So, on that special day of the sunspots, the memories of his past life came flooding back. It

96

was more than memories, more like his own life, and he was waking up from a long sleep to be the destined warrior he had survived for centuries to become. Now he knew he had been born to be a warrior. He was a warrior, and his name was Achilles, son of the goddess Thetis and descendant of the Olympian god, Poseidon.

There were still major gaps in his memory, but he knew he had been awaken now for battle. There were powers at his controls also, but they were sketchy. Thetis had given him her power to shape shift, but he couldn't remember how to use it. He sensed other powers, too, but those were also elusive. He needed help to remember, and he sensed others of his kind.

His mental awakening came even before he saw it manifested in his golden aura. It was a great and wonderful surprise to see the golden octopus covering and hovering over him. It was so appropriate that his aura was a sea creature.

George was trying to figure out how he could make contact with the others when he heard the news report about the glows being some kind of dementia caused by the sunspots. He knew instantly that the others were searching for him. He called the "Hot Line" immediately and was told a medical team (code word for the others) would be dispatched to him. All he had to do now was wait.

He watched anxiously for the others, knowing they would be here soon. They must have been close, because it really didn't take the vans all that long to get there. But, when the vans arrived he knew something was wrong. The occupants came pouring out of the van very much like a SWAT team launching on a target, and obviously he must be the target. The other thing he noticed was the horrible red aura they all had, nothing like his golden one. Another thing: even excluding their actions, he knew they were the enemy by the rage he felt swelling up inside him.

Unfortunately, he was alone, and they were many, at least twenty. So he did the only thing he could do. He ran like hell out the back door, and he was fast. As he busted out the back door he crashed directly into three of the enemy, knocking two of them down. He stood facing the last one and watched him pull out a sword from under his trench-coat. Fear flushed over him, but he never stopped moving. The two he knocked down were trying to get up, and he immediately kicked them under the chin, laying them out cold. He quickly picked up one of the swords they had dropped and stood to face the third. They circled each other fainting, and something seemed strange. The enemy seemed to move slow. This reminded him of a long forgotten power and tried to concentrate on that power, but he couldn't remember how to fully activate it. He had to get away and didn't have time to waste, so he attacked, blocking the enemies strike and brought his sword down at the base of the red devil's neck. He had killed his first enemy in this life, but as it fell he saw a wall of them coming at him. They were slow, but damn, there were a lot of them. He didn't have time to consider it and attacked. Two then four went down to his sword before he felt the searing pain rock his body over and over, but his last thoughts were rage, rage that he would not be joining his kin in the battles to come.

***

As Augie suspected, they had been watching and listening to her conversation with the FBI agent, Jack Ward, and when he gave Augie the three addresses, they sought out the first in the Miami area.

They were too late! The battle image formed within the mist to show a magnificent warrior standing against many demons, far too many to survive and far too late to save him. His golden aura was bright and took the form of a huge octopus. Zeus heard Poseidon gasp and saw him lean forward on his throne.

"Oh, no." said Poseidon, "That's one of mine. That's the son of the goddess Thetis, my daughter. That is Achilles, and one of the greatest warriors we have ever had. We must save him."

Even as Poseidon said the words, Achilles was stabbed in the back by several demons, then mutilated by a horde of the damn demons. Sadly, they watched the aura fade of what could have been their greatest warrior.

The image in the mist faded just as the Dark Angels arrived and darted into the mist. Zeus announce that they were too late to help the first on the list and was sending them to the address of the second. Hopefully, they would be in time to save this one.

After the Dark Angels left, they continued to monitor them, but they also grieved the loss of one of their own. There would be no need to share what they had seen with the team. After all, they didn't know Achilles and didn't need any extra stress. Like the others they had seen murdered, their grief would remain private.

***

The Dark Angels materialized this time in the front yard of a suburban home in Scottsdale, Arizona. The Angels quickly formed a defensive circle with Augie and Karrie in the center. Their protection seemed automatic, maybe because of her and Karrie's age (old and young), but more likely because of Augie's apparent mastery of the time alterations was a power that needed to be protected. At least she was now a welcomed member of the team. Karrie didn't even have a weapon, hell she was still somewhat in shock from her own rescue, but she wasn't about to be left out. Augie thought the real reason Karrie was here was because Heracles wasn't about to let her out of his sight. She chuckled to herself.

Seeing no danger, but after the last trap, they carefully surveyed the house and area. Looking safe, they approached the door, but the door opened before they reached it, and an elderly man in his mid-seventies stood looking at them with wide eyes and a bright golden image of a lion with full mane. He was apparently staring at the Angels' golden auras. He said, "What the hell?"

Augie stepped forward and said, "Sorry to startle you, but we have much to tell you and little time to do it. The most important thing you need to know right now is that you are in danger, and you must come with us to survive." Augie saw no one else inside and asked, "Do you live alone?"

"Yes, my wife died two years ago," he said.

Startled still, he did not resist her urging him out into the yard with them, nor did he react when they began to shimmer and disappear, just to reappear in the courtyard of an apartment complex in Harlingen, Texas. When the shimmering stopped, they were already standing in their defensive positions.

***

Seve Lopez always had a hard time keeping the smile off of his face, but truth be known, he didn't want too. He seemed to always be outgoing and happy, even with his sister, who seemed intent on wiping his smile away. At almost fourteen years old, he had always been happy.

When he first saw his aura he was beyond happy; he was thrilled. He was standing naked in the bathroom drying himself when he saw it ... a golden stag with an incredible rack of antlers, and it surrounded him. He thought, Wow, just wait until my football teammates at Memorial Middle School see this. I'm some kind of superhero. He was so excited that he forgot he was naked and ran into the living room screaming, "Look at this! Look at this!"

His sister screamed, then started laughing and said, "Get real, Seve."

His mother said, "I've seen it before, Seve."

Mortified, Seve covered himself and said, "No ... not that. Look at my golden glow ... my stag image."

His father said, "Oh, for Pete's sake, Seve. There's nothing glowing except your cheeks. Go put some clothes on."

They couldn't see it! Damn. What good is it to have this special glow if no one can see it. He was disappointed and even more so when no one at school noticed it either, which he attended for three more days. After three days still no one had noticed his glow. He was depressed enough to stop smiling ... almost.

On the fourth day he came home from school and was told by his father that he heard on the news about people that believe they have a glow should call in for treatment. He said he called the number and people were on their way to their apartment.

Only he and his father were home. His mother was still at work as a nurse, and his sister was off at college. For some uncomfortable reason he was glad they were gone.

He heard the doorbell ring and his father let them in. When he came into the living room his smile faded completely. Five really horrible looking men draped in bright red glows were staring, no snarling, at him, and the looks he was seeing reflected pure evil hate. They hated him. He didn't know why, but he knew he was in danger. He screamed. His father must have felt the evil and recognized the danger, because he jumped in between him and the five men and shoved him out the door and said, "Run, Seve!" That's exactly what he did. He ran faster than he had ever ran before, but before he sped away he saw his father bloody and falling, trying to block the door to give him time to get away.

***

When the Dark Angles materialized, screaming was coming from the second story, and they looked

102

up in time to see a boy with a golden aura sprinting down the stairs three at a time with five demons hot on his heels. The boy's golden aura took the shape of a male deer with huge antlers, and he seemed to be fleet on his feet as this apparition would denote. The boy saw the Angels and immediately turned to run directly toward them. There was no doubt that the boy already considered them friends or at least less of a threat. Heracles stepped to the side to let the boy run into the safety of the circle. He then stepped back to fill the gap with his huge body and waited. Augie raised her arms high into the air and the demons slowed. Heracles, although visibly seething with rage, smiled at the approaching demons as he stepped forward to engage them.

Although the demons were moving in slow motion, they were still moving and dangerous. The demons changed their strategy, however, and Augie watched in horror as the demons began pulling pistols out from under their trench-coats. The demons couldn't kill the Alpha spirits by shooting the human host, but they could certainly incapacitate them while they used their swords to kill them. She hadn't considered this option, but she should have anticipated the possibility. Her sudden fear strengthened her grip on time and slowed it further, just as two guns fired, but her timing was too late for Heracles. His closeness to the guns prevented him from reacting fast enough, and a bullet caught him in the stomach. He fell to the ground with a thud, but Asteria quickly stood over him and seemed to deflect the other bullet with her sword. By then Athena, in a rage, launched into the demons like a whirlwind, slicing and chopping

103

her way through them. The demons didn't get any more shots off, since they were missing their gun arms. Athena then went back through the screaming demons along with Asteria, who had now joined Athena in the battle. Together, they destroyed the attackers and their demons auras.

Ralph Henderson held the boy, who appeared to be about thirteen. Now momentarily safe, the boy began sobbing out, "They killed my father. My dad pushed me out the door and told me to run, while he fought them, but they killed him."

Hugging the boy, the old man said, "I'm sorry son. You are safe now. Your father saved you."

While the two Dark Angel warriors fought, Karrie screamed and ran to Heracles, who was on the ground holding his stomach in pain.

What happened then amazed them all. Karrie moved Heracles' hands from his wound and replaced them with her own. Her hands began to glow brightly blue over his wound for several minutes, and Heracles visibly began to slowly relax from his pain. The glow subsided and Karrie removed her hands to reveal that his wound was completely healed. Karrie handed him the bullet her hands had sucked from his stomach. Heracles stared at the bullet in wide-eyed disbelief, then at her and slowly stood up. He then smiled hugely and wrapped Karrie in his huge arms.

Augie said, "What did you do, Karrie?"

"I have no idea. I just suddenly remembered how," said Karrie.

By this time a crowd had gathered and was staring in wonder and pointing, and sirens could

also be heard in the not so distance.    Augie said,
"We better get the hell out of here."

Again the shimmering began and they saw the
shocked crowd wink out.

# Chapter 7
## Ancient Revelation

Zeus reveled in the Dark Angels' victories, and even more pleased in the newest raven haired Angel. At first he was horrified to see Heracles injured from the human technology. All the gods were concerned with the potential loss of their most powerful warrior, but when Karrie (Helen) ran forward, they all leaned forward in rapt attention, then they all began to smile when they recognized the healing, blue glow that emerged from her hands. She had demonstrated the power of healing, rare even among the entire Titan race.

Zeus asked, "Do any of you recognize this healer spirit?" No one spoke. The Olympians hadn't seen a healer in centuries, but they were certainly happy to see one now, especially engaged in this war. Helen had not been a healer, so part of her Alpha spirit must include other combined Alpha spirits. Unfortunately, that healing spirit could not be identified. In time maybe the spirit would reveal itself.

"We should have recognized her from her two snake aura, Hermes, after all it's the dual snakes, staff and wings symbol humans have been using for centuries to denote medical or healing. Don't you remember the staff for healing you made?"

Hermes said, "I remember the staff, but I was too busy fearing her aura to make any connection." The gods laughed.

So, the atmosphere around the chamber was pleasant, even jovial, as the warriors returned, but it didn't last long.

Augie launched immediately into a tirade as soon as they were all solid, "Well, we are now seven, no thanks to you gods. We have done more to save ourselves than anything you gods have done. All I see this Assembly doing is sitting on your asses staring into the mist. You're not teaching us about our powers or how to use them. All you seem to want to do is give us transportation. You tell us we are the warriors and we are in a war, but you don't seem to want to help us much. We almost got killed today in several ways, and you left it up to us to learn how to save ourselves."

Zeus was instantly angered. No one talked to him like that, and this was the second time! He sucked in a large lungful of air to bellow his rage, but Hera spoke first,

"Calm yourself, my husband. Relax that lightning bolt that I know you are about to launch. This lady Alpha is correct. From her and the other Alphas' perspectives we don't appear to be helping them. My husband, we must be more forthcoming with our charges. They deserve it, and they are our future. But, I must warn you, lady Alpha, don't show such disrespect again. I will not intervene again. I can assure you, we deserve respect."

For once Hera was correct. In fact she was more than correct. They needed these Alphas in more ways than one. "OK, Augie, you and the other Alphas deserve the complete truth."

Zeus began, "As we have explained before, Titans are immortal mostly because we are more energy than actual body. Ages ago we created bodies for our race of energy being, these bodies and others. We have already explained about the spirits and how they transfer and about the corruption of the soul. In order to save the Alpha spirits from destruction, you and the others, we poured our essence into the energy beam that caused your spirit to awaken. By saving you, we have doomed our immortal bodies. We, our immortal bodies and part of our spirit, are now dying, and we don't have much time left. We here of the Assembly have sacrificed ourselves so that you Alphas might live. You Alphas will eventually replace us on these thrones.

We hope your new race, yes, you are a new race of beings and, unlike us, will not be as dependent on the dais as we are, but your race must be capable of using its power. Augie, I believe you already are discovering its vast power. You must learn this power before we fade away, because our spirits will transfer and we will become Alphas in human form, and you must be ready to save us from the Omegas. So, you see, we are depending completely on you Alphas."

"We have not been ignoring you; we have been observing you and learning, because you are different. Our old ways are obsolete, and we must adapt if we are to survive. Most of us have already purged our Omega, so when we pass, only the Alpha will transfer. We will be like you and part of this new race, assuming you can save us from the hordes of Omega."

Augie said, "I'm so sorry. We didn't know how much you sacrificed to save us."

Zeus said, "We are very hesitant to teach you the old ways. We must let you learn the new ways...your ways."

*** 

The days were beginning to run together for Karrie, but one thing remained common to each new day ... fear. Each day brought new experiences and new fears. She had watched in horror as her parents had been killed in front of her, but she had been kept alive. She had somehow cheated death. At first she hoped for death to relieve the pain of the loss of her mother and father, but as she waited through the hours, her pain turned to a seething rage, boiling inside her. The demon men beat her for pleasure, but the explosion within awoke a part of her, and when she saw the others with the golden aura, she felt a connection even stronger than family, if that's possible. When she saw the huge warrior with the axe, she instantly knew him from long, long ago, and her mind surged with joy at seeing him. He knew her, too, but neither remembered when or how they knew each other. It didn't seem to matter; they were together again, and that's all that mattered.

Everything from that point was new, yet it was not new. When they appeared in Mount Olympus, she recognized it from ancient times. She had been here before, and she knew these gods, especially Aphrodite. Aphrodite called her Helen. Yes, that seemed right. Hell, it was too confusing, but one thing she knew for sure: she belonged here with these other Dark Angels, and if they were going to fight the red demons, she definitely was going to join them.

She remembered in the depths of her mind that she had once had powers, but she couldn't remember what they were. When she went into her first engagement, Athena had given her a sword, but it didn't feel right. It wasn't until Heracles was suffering in pain that she remembered her power. She cared for Heracles in ways that she didn't understand. It was like they were two halves of a single entity, and when his pain radiated out to her, she remembered. Her empathy for his pain drained into her and she felt his pain. She absorbed his pain and wound into herself through her brightly glowing blue hands. Once she owned the injury and felt the pain as hers, her body generated a counter energy that corrected the injury and expelled the pain from both of them. Yes, she remembered this power; it involved energy. It was only part of a more complex power of empathy.

She was pleased with herself and greatly relieved that Heracles was now whole again. Heracles seemed surprised, searching his stomach for the bullet-hole and finding none, and the other Dark Angels were visibly shocked and greatly pleased with her abilities. In that moment Helen truly became a contributing and welcome member of the Dark Angels, even though she really knew very little about who they were. The others tried to explain to her, but it really didn't matter. She belonged, and she would stay. This was now her life.

When they returned to Mount Olympus, she thought Augie pressed her luck with Zeus by insulting the gods. Helen, yes, she was Helen now, sensed that Zeus was on the verge of losing his temper, but then Zeus always seemed to be at that point. Helen intervened slightly to calm his fury, while Hera spoke. If Zeus noticed her involvement, he didn't make it known.

Afterwards, Helen was glad that Augie had pushed. Zeus' revelation was extremely informative for all of them, and it actually brought the gods and Angels closer together, but it was probably a little too much information for the elderly, Mr. Henderson to process. He was absorbing all the information, but he had little to build on. It would come soon enough.

# Chapter 8
# Earth Fights Back

Jack Ward worked directly with Director Setliff for the next two days, which were extremely busy. He and the director stayed together and under guard, taking naps in shifts to get through the ordeal. After re-establishing communications, Director Setliff called the US Attorney General to inform him of a national terror threat and request his support to brief the other intelligence agencies. He was afraid to tell him everything up front until he was first able to declare the FBI clear. This was his number one priority, but before he could do that he had to consolidate power and cooperation between some of the other intelligence agencies. Director Setliff called the directors of the CIA and NSA and called for an immediate top-secret meeting at his secure facility, the only one.

Within two hours the directors of the CIA, NSA and the AG were escorted into Director Setliff's secure conference room to join them and the FBI Director Mosley from Quantico, who had arrived just before them. It was a top-secret meeting, but all three of those arriving brought their aides with them. The director was instantly pissed that they presumed to assume the aides would be welcome, since they knew this was top-secret. The aides were undoubtedly cleared for top-secret, but it was a presumption the director wasn't going to allow. Just as he was about to explode, Jack squeezed his arm and handed him the glasses. Jack had been wearing the glasses when the guests walked in and had already noticed that the aide to the CIA director was a demon. Even worse, the Attorney General was also a demon.

Director Setliff looked at Jack and simply whispered, "Crap! OK, this means they must stay. Hell, it will make it easier to explain anyway. This should be fun."

Jack dialed his second and told him to bring a security team and come to the conference room. Five minutes later Jim Taylor led in a ten man security team who immediately lined the walls and waited.

The Attorney General, the demon, barked, "Okay, we're here now. What's all the mystery about?"

Director Setliff played it smart. He reached under the table and activated the security system for the room, then said, "Well, gentlemen and lady, since the aide to the CIA Director was female, I'll make this simple. We have found ourselves in the middle of a war between aliens, a war in which Earth has apparently already lost!"

The AG's eyes bugged for a split second before he recovered and said, "That's ridiculous!"

"I wish I was wrong, but I'm not. The infiltrators are called Omegas, and they radiate a horrific red aura ... kind of like the one you are generating along and your friend there at the CIA!" At the mention of Omegas and auras the AG knew he had been busted and jumped to his feet in an uncontrollable rage and launched himself across the table directly toward him. The director wasn't expecting a direct attack, but the security guards were prepared. The guard knew it was true, having

113

looked through the glasses himself and helped capture some of the other demons. The guard caught the AG in the forehead with his rifle butt and knocked him out cold on the table. The other Omega was slower and didn't have a chance to move before the guards subdued her.

The Director of the CIA jumped to his feet and bellowed, "Director Setliff, I demand to know what the hell is going on and right now!"

Director Setliff held his hands up to calm the CIA Director, handed him the sunglasses and said, "Be calm, Director Shepard. You will understand soon, but take a look through these glasses. It will make the story shorter."

Director Shepard skeptically took the glasses and slipped them on, just to yank them off again. He tried the glasses several time, handed them to Director Mosley, then said, "Alright, I'm listening. Tell me the story."

Director Setliff ordered the security team to take the two demons and place them in detention with the other demons they had captured, then activated the conference room security again before he began. Director Setliff began the story at the beginning, allowing Deputy Director Ward to fill in the story prior to his notification, then added the facts and actions since he became aware. When he finished, the room was utterly silent for many long moments.

Director Shepard said, "What do you propose we do now? You do realize that you just arrested the Attorney General of the United States? People will miss him."

114

Director Setliff said, "Well, that is part of the problem. According to the Alphas, the world and most governments have been infiltrated by them, as evidenced by your own aide. I found five of the damn demons just in this FBI headquarters facility. I suppose getting our own agencies cleansed is the first order of business. That is why I have Director Mosley here. Quantico will be my next order of business. After Quantico is clear, I will move these demons down there and make it the new headquarters for this operation. From there we can get our Behavioral Analysis team working to profile the demons. We have to find a way to find and identify them."

"Are you kidding me?" screamed Director Shepard, "We have to keep all this secret, at least until we have the military brought into the loop. What if the military is ordered to attack us? Think about it. We want them on our side, and we don't know how much the Omegas already control. Knowing this, and you want to move the operation to Quantico? No way! You don't have that good of security there. I mean the FBI facility at Quantico is in the middle of the largest and most active Marine Corp base in the world. You have military protection but just one of the demons hiding out will alert all the rest. It will take days, if not weeks, to secure the Marine base."

"No, Sir. Let's move the operation to the CIA headquarters at Langley. Langley is isolated, maintains its own extremely high security, can easily be locked down and secured, and push comes to shove, will be easier to monitor and defend, if necessary."

"I agree that the FBI Behavioral Analysis team is an excellent idea. They are the best in the world to profile the demons, but we can temporally move them to Langley."

Director Setliff analyzed what he had heard and said, "Yes, that makes sense. Cleansing the CIA should be the next move then. We already know you have Omegas within your organization." After another moment of thought he said "Let's do it. Then, I suppose, we move on to the military intelligence agencies. We will definitely need to make sure the military is not compromised. Like you suggest, we don't know how far they have infiltrated our government, but we have to protect the president, and I'm thinking Camp David, assuming ..."

Director Shepard finished his sentence, "Assuming the president isn't one of them. I could easily believe that ass hole is one. Damn, this could really get complicated. Another thing, the president will have to wait until we secure the military's support. I'm sorry Director Campbell, but NSA, you, needs to be with us for the time being. I mean, you stay with us until we can move on D.C. to cleanse it. We can't take a risk of this secret getting out until we can get organized, and you know politicians can't keep a secret. Secrets leak out there faster than anywhere."

"I suppose I don't have a choice in this decision?" said Director Campbell.

Directors Setliff and Shepard said in unison, "NO!"

Director Shepard said, "I assume that you don't know who is controlling the aliens or where their headquarter is?"

"Hell no!" said Director Setliff, "We just became aware of the full problem today, but right now we have an advantage, because they don't know we can identify them with these glasses."

"Speaking of these glasses," Director Shepard said, "Can we replicate the glasses? We will need more of them."

Jack Ward spoke up, "The Alpha, Augie, said they couldn't be duplicated, but we have the best optic technology and experts at Quantico. We will try, and I might be able to get more from Augie."

Director Campbell said, "These other aliens, you called Alphas, how do you know we can trust them? How do you know they are the good guys?"

Jack Ward answered, "As I have said, they teleported me there. I have no idea where, but they wanted me to see them with my own eyes for a reason. I think they wanted me to see their technology to let me know their power. It was certainly more than what we have. If they wanted to destroy us, I don't think we could stop them. Their fear is of the Omega. They told me their time, the Omega, had come and they intend to take over the world and enslave humans. They also said the Omegas would destroy them as well. The Alphas intend to fight them, but I don't think there are many of them, and there are apparently tens of thousands of the Omegas, judging by what we have seen so far. They will need our help, and I think we will need theirs."

After only two rings, Augie said, "Hello, Jack. What's up?"

Jack gave her a brief overview of the activities on his end and soliciting the help of the CIA. He also felt it significant to tell her about the Attorney General being a demon and how infiltrated he suspected the government must be. He finally got to the reason for the call and said, "We have a split operation with trying to clear out the CIA of demons and cleansing the FBI Quantico operation, so we can use those location as our joint headquarters. Once we are completely operational and secure at Quantico, hopefully, we can analyze the glasses and build more. Maybe we can also find something by profiling the demons and DNA analysis, but we need to become operational without the demons knowing. I loaned the CIA director the glasses. Can you help us with more of those glasses or possibly loan us an Alpha?"

"What are you going to do with the Omegas you have captured?" Augie asked.

"We are going to take them to the CIA headquarters at Langley and interrogate and study them," Jack said.

Augie thought for a minute and said, "That is fine for a while, but then you must turn them over to us. They must be destroyed by us. Do you understand?"

"Yes, we understand, but we need to study them first."

Augie said, "Alright, we will give you some time but not long. They are dangerous. They may even have powers we aren't yet aware of. I will check on the glasses, but I was told they cannot be

118

duplicated. Maybe we can get you a few more glasses from the Olympian gods. I will check. In the meantime we will provide you with an Alpha, a liaison between you and us, to give you some help, but you must protect the Alpha. The Omegas will stop at nothing to kill us."

"Yes, I understand."

Augie said, "Meet me at the park in four hours, on your way to Quantico." Then she was gone.

\*\*\*

Augie didn't really know how much authority she had among the Olympians, but she had the distinct impression that the Olympian gods were pushing the Alphas to take over. If so, she would take over, part of the operation anyway. Damn, she still had so much to learn.

She went to the Assembly and briefed them on the activities with the humans and their efforts to find the Omegas and their request for more glasses to help them.

Zeus and the other gods listened intently, but she got the impression they didn't understand fully the human activities and efforts, but they accepted the fact that she did. They seemed willing to do what she suggested, but Zeus said, "There are some things you still don't understand, so I will be honest with you. Our strength is beginning to wane. Soon we will be no more. Creating the magic you desire will sap what remaining strength we have, strength we hope to save for use in the teleportations. Another fact that you need to know: we don't know what powers you may or may not have as Alphas. We will only know as you succeed in awakening them."

Augie truly began to understand and said, "Thank you for your honesty. We will attempt to begin helping the Assembly." She then dismissed herself and called a meeting of the Alphas.

As they gathered in her room, she began relaying all she knew to the other Alphas, even her experiments with the dais in her room. When she finished, she said, "We have to learn how to become the gods of the Assembly, or, quite frankly, we will die with the Olympians. The way I see it, we must help the FBI wage the battle for Earth against the Omegas. We are too few, and the Omegas are many, and they have had centuries to infiltrate everywhere. As the gods have said, they are complete and ready to take over Earth, and they will as soon as they have eliminated us. We and the knowledge we possess are the only things they fear. If the Omegas discover we are teaching the FBI about them and how to kill them, I'm afraid they will attack the FBI, CIA or anyone else they might suspect. We must keep this a secret and help them as much as possible."

"I will attempt to make a few more of the glasses. I was successful with the cell-phone magic, maybe I can succeed with the glasses, but I think we need someone on the inside at the FBI, someone that can identify the demons. Mr. Henderson, I think that needs to be you. I know you're new and not fully attuned to the situation, but we can't spare a warrior, and the children are too young."

"I understand completely," said Mr. Henderson, "I will do whatever I can. Whether I like it or not, I'm part of the team now."

Augie hadn't been able to spend much time with Mr. Henderson, but she liked his attitude. Evidently, he had been a college professor for forty years, teaching history, biology and science, and even though he was her senior by ten years and completely white headed, he was still a fine looking man. He was tall and bronzed from the Arizona sun, and although elderly, he certainly wasn't frail but was definitely on the downside of his physical prime.

The Mexican boy, Seva, he called himself, had stuck close to Mr. Henderson after he had been rescued but had recently begun to buddy with Sue, since they were of the same approximate age. So, Mr. Henderson truly was the best choice and wise of worldly ways.

Augie didn't have much time to delve into her dais, but try as she did, was unable to create another pair of glasses. Failing that, she didn't even try to create another cell-phone. But, she had detected emotions radiating from Mr. Henderson's mind like she had with Asteria, which she believed could eventually develop into telepathic communications, at least the basics seemed to exist. It was the best she could do for the time being.

It had been a little over four hours and before she left the dais, she observed Jack Ward in the park waiting. She took Mr. Henderson to the Assembly for teleport. Originally, she had intended to meet Jack there and make introductions, but to save the Assembly's remaining energy she decided to just teleport Mr. Henderson there. It wasn't like that many people would materialize in Pershing Park, so Jack would make the connection quickly enough.

***

Jack Ward was standing in the park with directors Setliff and Mosley waiting when Mr. Henderson materialized beside them. It startled both directors, but Jack welcomed the shock. It reinforced the believability of the situation. Jack said, "I'm Jack Ward. I assume Augie sent you?"

Mr. Henderson said, "Yes, I am Ralph Henderson, the Alpha sent to help you. I might also suggest that you quickly get me into your van and out of sight. The enemy doesn't need to see my aura."

"Yes, of course," Jack said.

They rapidly got into the black SUV with tinted windows, but before they left to lead the precession of identical SUV toward Langley, Mr. Henderson said, "Mr. Ward, in an abundance of caution please have all of the occupants of the other SUVs show themselves. I want to clear them."

Jack was confident of all the other occupants, but he liked Mr. Henderson's caution and complied with his request. It only took a few moments and Mr. Henderson was satisfied and more comfortable during the trip.

Mr. Henderson tried to answer most of the question they bombarded him with during the trip, but him being so new, he wasn't much help. They were also surprised that Mr. Henderson was one of the Alphas recently rescued from the FBI "Hot Line".

The trip wasn't that long, and as they pulled up to the CIA security gate at Langley, Mr. Henderson surprised them again when he said, "The guard

122

about to check us is an Omega!" Then he quickly crouched to the floor and covered his head.

Jack knew they would be finding demons today, but he wasn't expecting it so soon. He, however, reacted immediately and ordered the leading SUV to capture and subdue the guard, which they quickly did without the guard knowing there was an Alpha present. They were also lucky that the large prisoner bus was a few miles behind them. This Omega guard would have surely reported it, and all their plans would have been destroyed. As it was now, the guard joined them.

Director Shepard said, "Well this is as good a time as any. Let's put Langley under full lockdown and communication blackout!" They waited, however, just long enough for the prisoner bus carrying the Omegas to come through, pick up its newest prisoner, and proceed on to the detention holding area.

The search began first at the other security gates at Langley, then they alerted the full on base security team to form in the yard, where Mr. Henderson could check them all at once. Once the ranks were formed, Mr. Henderson exited the van and began checking the ranks. He had gone about half-way through the ranks when they heard a blood curdling scream erupt from the ranks, and a low crouching guard in the back burst from the ranks running toward Mr. Henderson. At seeing the golden aura, the demon lost all rational thought. Its sole thought was destruction of the Alpha. Mr. Henderson's security team leaped in front of him as a shield, and sadly, two of them took bullets before the demon could be subdued. Luckily, they had been wearing protective vests and only one was seriously wounded in the leg.

That attack had been the only remaining demon among the resident security team. Afterward, the cleared guards were positioned around the courtyard and parking lots and emergency evacuation alarms were sounded. As the workers emerged from the buildings they were ushered into a manageable area in one of the large parking lots, where Mr. Henderson could observe them. He wasn't allowed to get close to the crowd, but he was able to identify three more demons. The security team was able to dissect the unarmed demons from the crowd without more than a scuffle. Afterwards, they systematically searched the cars and buildings floor by floor and room by room, anywhere one of the demons could have hidden. This inspection had been a total surprise to the demons and they hadn't been prepared to evade detection, so no more demons were found.

By the time the area was secured, the FBI Behavior Analysis team from Quantico had arrived at the front gate. After screening them they were allowed to enter and begin their investigation, interrogation of the demons and profiling.

# Chapter 9
# The Angels' Powers Grow

Aphrodite touched Augie's mind to summon her and the Dark Angels. Again she whistled for the team, and they gathered and approached the Assembly.

Zeus said, "We have found more Alphas ... two of them, twins in Japan. They are in the open, but they don't seem to be in immediate danger. We can't count on this to continue. Please hurry into the mist."

As they hurried into the mist of the dais, she had to stop Sue and Seva, saying, "Sorry kids. You two better stay." They looked disappointed but complied and stepped out of the mist, but as the image began to sparkle, she noticed the two kids look at each other with a mischievous twinkle in their eyes and a quick grin. What were these two up to? Whatever it was she would have to wait for their return to find out.

As now customary, they appeared in their defensive posture in an open area near a street market in the outskirts of Tokyo, Japan. The denseness of the crowd prevented a teleport any closer to the twins, but they swiftly identified their location about a half block into the market. The racial makeup of the Dark Angels and their goth manner of dress and heavy armament made them stand out in the crowd. All their weapons, with the exception of Heracles' axe, which he carried low, were sufficiently covered by their black trench-coats, but still they did not blend in well. Of course, part of it was the intensity of their appearance and rigid posture as they pursued the two Japanese youth, but the crowd began to spread out, clearing their advancement. The building silence proceeding the Dark Angels alerted the two youths. They turned to stare first at each other then back to the approaching group. They did not seem to be frightened or intimidated, but they remained cautious, poised to run if necessary.

Since Augie was the least intimidating of the team, she motioned the others to wait as she slowly approached and said, "Do you speak English?"

They both responded in English, finishing each other's sentences, "Yes, we speak English. Most of the younger Japanese do. Who are you? Why do you glow golden? Do you know why we also glow?"

Once she was closer she realized they were younger than she originally thought. They were obviously twins, a boy and a girl, of about fifteen years old, but they were both radiating an exceeding strong and large aura, and both auras were shaped identically in the form of golden gorillas. The gorillas looked misshapen in that the shoulders were overly wide and the large muscular arms and huge hands hung down the sides of these youth, almost down to their knees ... very intimidating in appearance.

Augie said, "Yes, I can answer your questions, but I need to tell you first that you are in danger. We are the Dark Angels of Zeus, and we have come to protect you. Both of you are part of us, kin. You must come with us, now before we are attacked."

The twins said, "Are you talking about the...," they spoke together in Japanese then together said, "Demons?"

"Yes, you have seen them?"

"Yes!" they said, "We have fought them."

Augie was about to say that she was surprised that they were still alive, but Athena interrupted her to say, "It's too late. They are coming, now."

When she looked up there was a wave of red aura demons coming toward them roughly pushing aside the crowd. Athena led them out of the market into an area of open space where they positioned themselves for battle. Augie instinctively led the twins into the protected area behind the Dark Angels with her and began pulling energy within herself. By the time the line of scores of demons closed on them, she raised her arms to grasp time. This time she grasp hard on time and surrounded her team with an umbrella of this radiated energy. The army literally froze in mid-stride and mid-attempts to fire weapons. There were a few puffs of smoke indicating guns had been fired, but the bullets came slowly, allowing the Angels to dodge them or bat them down. After that, the battle was total mayhem. It was like cutting wheat with a scythe. Heads were falling in every direction as Heracles, Athena, and Asteria charged into the line of demons. Helen jumped in to fill the defensive position armed with a sword, but what surprised her most was the actions of the twins.

The twins jumped into the fray with no weapons at all. They ran and rolled under and between the demons, and the huge golden hands of the gorillas became their weapons, ripping off heads

127

as they came within reach of the instruments of death. All the twins had to do was to move their weapons within reach of more heads. Their auras seemed to solidify and come alive, and the rage bellowed out from them. They were awesome to watch, even the other Dark Angels slowed their assault to admire the work of the twins. The twins were instantly accepted as warriors.

Jointly the Dark Angels completed the destruction of the demon army in what must have appeared to have happen in a flash to those humans gathered. With time effectively sped up for the Dark Angels, they must have appeared almost invisible to the watchers, while to the Dark Angels the world moved in extreme slow motion.

With the engagement over and won, Augie released her grip on time and the world moved back to its normal pace. This seizure on time had been her strongest yet. Her power was definitely growing, like the rest of them. They were becoming a smooth operating team, and the twins meshed in perfectly.

Once the time spell relaxed the crowd began screaming at the suddenly appearing carnage, which made her take a second look. There was blood everywhere, broken and mutilated bodies lay sprawled all over the lawn, but the most frightening sight was the lifeless heads all around, staring at nothing. The crowd was terrified and ran in every direction, leaving the Dark Angels alone in the middle of the carnage, watching the red demons withering and fading into obscurity.

Augie suddenly remembered that she had told the twins they were in danger. She laughed at herself for making that assumption: that the twins were helpless. They said they had fought them before. They were far from helpless, but the fact remained that, had the Dark Angels not been there, the twins would have been overwhelmed and killed by the sheer volume of demon warriors attacking. They realized this also.

Augie got back to where they were before the attack, answering the twin's questions. She said, "Yes, we came to protect you from the demons. We glow because we are all descendants of an ancient race, just like you, and we are all under attack and must band together."

The twins responded using their sing song back and forth joint statement, "We believe you, and accept your offer. Nothing is keeping us here. We live in an orphanage and have no family. One thing, though, the police will come soon. We better leave."

Augie agreed and notified Aphrodite to retrieve them.

\*\*\*

Ever since Augie described her experience dealing with the dais, Seva had wanted to get involved. As long as he could remember he had explored the fascinating and challenging complexities of computers, not how they work, but all the various uses they could be put to. He started by playing video games in every imaginable version but quickly moved on to the vast world of the internet and its personal challenges, and he loved to be challenged. His parents constantly told him he spent too much time on the computer, but it was far more interesting and mentally challenging than playing baseball or football. Now, since he couldn't go with the Dark Angels, he was drawn like a magnet to the dais, his ultimate challenge. This would be his opportunity to contribute to the team, and, surprisingly, Sue was almost as excited and wanted to help also. When they were left behind, although disappointed, they saw this as their opportunity to play and literally ran to Augie's dais.

All they had to go on was what Augie had told them, work backwards and let your mind be the keyboard and mouse. That sounded simple enough, but they couldn't even figure out how to turn it on.

Frustrated, Seva sat down in the only ... was it a stone throne? Yes, that word fit. The dais was in the corner and small, and there was only enough room for one chair ... throne, so Sue stood behind him with her hands on his shoulders, watching. He let his mind enter the dais, and immediately a mist flooded the dais. It felt like it was waiting for his instructions, so he began thinking about what and how to give it instructions. Still frustrated, he wished there were two thrones. Suddenly, the mist began to boil out of the dais and filled the room with thick smoke, blinding them. At first he thought he broke something, but he then felt movement around him and was afraid to move. Sue's hands squeezed painfully into his shoulders until the smoke returned into the dais.

As the room cleared, they looked around and couldn't believe their eyes. Augie's room had increased substantially in size to accommodate a larger dais and a second throne. Seva and Sue ran to the adjacent quarters to see if they had been destroyed, but to their surprise they looked untouched and normal, as if space had simply increased only in Augie's room.

Seva said, "Wow!" That pretty well summarized the situation.

Sue said, "Yeah. The gods did say something about the dais controlling matter. They also said humans only understand it as magic. I guess that is what happened ... magic."

They ran back into Augie's room and took their thrones. This time they both projected their minds into the mist, which seemed to immediately join in common thought. They became a common mind.

They jointly decided to try and complete what they came here to do, create more aura revealing sunglasses. As Augie had said, they worked backwards imagining the glasses identifying auras. The mist began to churn and concentrate, then form into a pair of glasses. The sunglasses hovered in the mist until Seva reached out and took them. The whole process took only a few minutes from beginning to end product. They continued building glasses until they had ten, five black pair and five pink pair, sue had to get her touch included. They decided that should be enough for now. Building the glasses became monotonous and boring, and they wanted to move on and do other things. This was just too exciting.

The next thing they created was something like a radio. They wanted music. Since there was no electricity, what they got was something that looked like a radio that tuned into the internet, but it was totally magic. It worked, that was the important thing.

By this time they were tired. Floating in the mist was draining, but they were also hungry, not for the bland and healthy food of Olympus. They wanted junk food. Before leaving the dais they created hamburgers, fries, and pizza, complete with the McDonald's wrappers and Pizza Hut boxes. To wash it down they created a case of coke.

After stuffing themselves they lay down on Augie's bed and were sound asleep when the Dark Angels returned.

***

Zeus and the assembly watched in awe as the battle took place in Japan. They didn't expect the twins aura to take active shape and actually fight. In the early days after the Titans created their forms, many had temporarily changed. He himself had flown as an eagle form. Other times he had changed into a lightning bolt to destroy his enemies, but this ... this symbiotic relationship was completely unexpected. It was, however, pleasantly welcome. This team of twins made incredible warriors.

As the Dark Angels appeared in the mist, Zeus welcomed them with a smile and said, "Welcome back my Angels. You are becoming an awesome team of warriors."

"As with many of you, I recognize your inhabiting Titan spirit, but some I don't. I do not recognize the spirits of these new warriors. What are you called?"

As was apparently their custom the twins said together, "Kazuo .... Kazue"

Zeus tried to say the names but failed terribly in frustration. He couldn't quite get his mouth around

132

the foreign names and said, "We will call you by other names."

Athena quickly offered, "How about we call them Jack and Jill?" Everyone chuckled at the names, but everyone instantly knew these names would stick." They would now be Jack and Jill, whether they liked it or not.

"Father," Athena said, marking the first time she, as a Dark Angel, in reality used that name, "All the Alphas so far are from America and now Japan. Why have we not found any Alphas in the other continents?"

It was Hera that spoke, "Titan genetic descendants were naturally concentrated around Greece, the original site of Mount Olympus. This means northeastern Africa, southwestern Asia, and southern Europe, what humans call the Mid-East. Even today, these descendants remain numerous there. This makes these areas the most active and populous for potential Alpha and Omega spirits. Unfortunately, these areas are ancient and Omega has apparently been active there virtually since the beginning. The awakened Alphas wouldn't have much of a chance to survive with the high population of Omegas, and we suspect that Omegas have been able to identify dormant Alphas in some way and kill them. For this reason most of these central countries are lost to us.

Finding Alphas in Japan was a surprise, because the indigenous population of Asia and South America remain mostly genetically pure and absent any Titan genetic influence. Apparently, however, some genetic mixing came to Japan after World War II from the American military."

133

"North America, in contrast, is a relatively new developing continent that received much of its initial population from Europe where the Titan spirits are less populous and more rare. While America obviously has a substantial population of descendants of Titan genetics, they are spread wider, and the Alphas there had a better chance of survival."

"We are currently searching Canada and northern Europe for survivors."

" I hope this helps."

Annoyed with Hera's interruption, Zeus spoke quickly to again gain control of the conversation, "You Alphas are becoming an amazement to us ... all of you. Wait until you see what the young ones have done. I think you will be surprised."

***

Augie thought Zeus looked mischievous with that smile, and when they entered her quarters, she was sure of it. As the kids had done, Augie stopped and looked outside, then back inside. The stone walls and everything else within had expanded or increased in size and shape inside her quarters, yet everything outside looked the same. She understood now why the Olympians called it magic; it's the only way humans would understand. They probably didn't understand how it worked either; it just did.

The kids were sound asleep on her bed surrounded by coke cans and pizza boxes, and she knew instantly that they had created them within the mist. Yes, they had learned. Obviously, they had also expanded her room and dais in the process.

134

Then she noticed the stack of sunglasses. Her chest swelled with pride at these two's accomplishments.

Jack and Jill picked up a slice of pizza and started eating, and the others quickly followed their example with pizza or cokes. With the renewed activity and noise in the room, Seve and Sue quickly awakened and started chattering excitedly about what they had discovered, and they certainly had a right to be excited.

All were interested in what the kids had done and listened intently, all except Heracles. He hadn't gotten any pizza and when they got to that part, he said, "Show us how to get more pizza, and if you don't mind, put some pepperoni on it." At that they all burst out in laughter.

Seve and Sue jumped up and went to the dais and took their seats, but Augie joined them this time. Seve saw her coming and duplicated his previous thoughts about another throne chair. Before she even reached them, the mist was boiling out of the dais and filling the room. When the room cleared again there was another throne chair, and the dais and room had expanded again. Amazed, Augie began clapping her hands, but Heracles said, "Don't forget the pizza!" Again they all burst out in laughter, but pizza boxes were already forming within the mist and hovering in front of Seve. With a big smile, he took the boxes and handed them to the hungry Heracles.

Augie took her seat and immediately felt her mind mingle with Seve and Sue. It was a little disorienting initially, but it quickly passed. She realized that the power of the dais increased exponentially with the number of users and now understood how and why the assembly of gods joined continually around their dais. This could be and probably was addictive to the Olympians. Without understanding exactly how she knew, she also realized that the power was coming from the users and that the dais was not a magic pool of mist.; It was an extension of the users.

As they were joined, she led the three of them on the journey to track Jack Ward and Mr. Henderson, and since their minds were joined, there was no communication required. What one thought, they all at the dais understood. As before, their minds raced through space and homed in to their exact location. Somewhat surprised, they soon found their joint mind hovering over Jack Ward and Mr. Henderson in the CIA headquarters at Langley and not at Quantico where she had expected.

As it was, they were just outside the bars of the detention facilities of the growing number of Omegas imprisoned, and the red demons were in an extremely agitated condition, flinging themselves at the bars trying to reach Mr. Henderson's Alpha spirit. It seemed to be an experiment and demonstration to the others, which she assumed were other directors.

Augie thought about Jack Ward's phone and it rang. He was sitting at a desk and answered immediately, "Yes, Jack Ward. Augie?"

"Yes," she said, "We are going to try something. We are sending you more glasses, but they haven't been tested yet. Clear the desk."

They watched as Jack quickly shoved the desk clear, while she took the glasses from Asteria. She placed them in the mist, where they continued to hover after she let them go. Together they projected a thought to transport the glasses to the desk. The sunglasses began to shimmer then disappear, as the shimmering began above the desk and finally fell to the desktop with a clatter. All eyes at that end were wide with wonder and amazement.

Jack quickly picked up a pair, careful not to grab one of the pink ones, and slipped them on to gaze at Mr. Henderson then the demons and said, "They work great. Thanks. These will be a great help to us here."

Augie said, "I think we can get you more, but it's been a long day for us. We now have a young team here to help, probably tomorrow." She winked at Seve and Sue and continued, "Jack, we need to expand our search for Alphas to Great Britain and Israel. We think there could be some surviving Alphas in those locations. If there are any, they will be there. Can you help us?"

"Yes, we have contacts in MI-5 and Mossad," Jack said.

Jack immediately shared their conversation with FBI Director Setliff and CIA Director Shepard, and after a brief conversation Director Shepard punched up his counterpart at MI-5's private direct line. After a single ring the MI-5 Chief answered, and Director Shepard said only a single word, "Quicksilver!"

The MI-5 Chief said, "Understood," and promptly hung up.

Afterwards, Director Shepard said, "I hope they are clear. Oh well, I've already declared 'Quicksilver'. With that call MI-5 and Mossad are already on their way here. We'll just have to deal with it, and hope we don't start a war in the process.

Jack said, "Hell, we apparently already have a war ... with the Omega.

# Chapter 10
# The Intelligence Community

As usual, most of the Dark Angels were in her expanded quarters discussing different subjects. One of the subjects now being discussed was how the twins' auras had fought for them against the demons. This interested her greatly, because her golden bear aura would make a fantastic weapon for her if she could figure out how to activate and use it.

The twins said, "We really don't know how our auras became active. Of course we had noticed each other's auras and had been experimenting with them. We kept it quiet, because we seemed to be the only ones in the orphanage that had them. In an orphanage you don't want to stand out.

After a while we learned that we could direct our auras, and with a little practice, learned to control and manipulate them as if they were second arms, at least that is the way it feels. We were lucky that we had, because one day we were sent to the market and some of the demons came at us with swords. Our auras seemed to come alive on their own and fought back and destroyed the demons. We were frightened and ran away and snuck back into the orphanage and hid. You came the second time we went out. The demons had gathered an army this time to kill us. Thank you, by the way."

Just as Augie was about to start experimenting with her aura, Mr. Henderson telepathically spoke to her mind, "Augie? Can you hear me?"

"Yes, Mr. Henderson. I hear you," Augie mentally transmitted.

"Please, Mr. Henderson sounds too formal. Call me Ralph. I thought you might be able to hear me, because I hear you sometimes. Anyway, they are about to have a top level meeting here at the CIA headquarters, and I thought you might like to watch. These agencies have been very busy, and I'm sure you would like to hear the results at this meeting."

"You bet I would! Thanks." Augie transmitted.

Augie quickly informed the others, including a mental transmission to Aphrodite, but most of the warriors were more interested in the aura discussion. Seve, Sue and even Karrie came to join her at the dais. Augie chuckled and said, "Time to expand the dais again."

Soon the four of them stared into the mist, joined minds and raced off in space. Seconds later they hovered invisible over the super secure conference room at the CIA headquarters. She then thought, This is silly. We didn't have to travel; we could have brought the meeting to us to view in the dais. Oh, well, next time.

It was a large conference room with many chairs and most were already full. Thankfully, there were seating placement signs on the table to let them know the participants. There were two seats for each agency plus those she already knew. Even Mr. Henderson had a placement representing (The Assembly) at the table, although he was not yet there. As she followed the seating signs she saw Air Force Intelligence, Army Intelligence, Coast Guard Intelligence, Marine Corps Intelligence,

140

Navy Intelligence, Chief MI-5, Massad, and in amazement she noticed a placement for the president and VP. There were a lot of agencies conspicuously missing, but all those present represented only extremely high security agencies, agencies trusted by the FBI and CIA. Augie also noticed heavily armed security guards aligning the walls and turned toward the inside, all of them wearing the special glasses, some pink. She heard Sue giggle. The FBI had apparently been able to duplicate the magic of the Olympians, because there was also a stack of them on the table in front of Director Setliff.

She already knew why guards were in the room. Among the group seated were demons. This explained the absence of Mr. Henderson ... Ralph. The last to be led into the room were the president and vice-president and four Secret Service agents, and she was shocked to see another demon, but thankfully only one.

The CIA Director took center stage at the podium and began, "I am sorry for all the cloak and dagger security, but you will all learn soon enough that we, all of us, our agencies have been penetrated and we are a breath away from losing it all. This agency, the CIA, here at any rate, has been cleansed and the major part of the FBI, here in Virginia at any rate, also, but your agencies are still at imminent risk."

The Director of Naval Intelligence stood and said, "Who is this enemy?"

Director Shepard said, "Vice Admiral, I am about to show you! Security, secure your prisoners."

The security guards immediately seized the Director of Army Intelligence, the Assistant Director of Air Force Intelligence, the Assistant Chief of MI-5, and lastly the President and one of his Secret Service agents. Before they knew it they had been stood against the wall together under gunpoint, and other security turned to squelch the chaos beginning around the table, forcing the remainder back in their chairs.

Director Shepard said, "Calm down and listen to me. Now, please, the rest of you slip on these glasses and look around the room."

There was an outpouring of grumbles, outrage and protests, but there was also a mixture of curiosity, and they took the sunglasses and slipped them on. The reaction was immediate and predictable. The glasses went on and off a few times, then the predictable questions and expletives.

Augie saw their mistake immediately and said, "Twins, I need you in the mist immediately."

They looked startled but jumped to comply. As soon as they were in the mist she directed their joint mind to teleport the twins into the conference room. She really didn't know how to teleport, but she didn't have time to learn. She trusted the dais to interpret her need. As they began to shimmer she said, "Kill the Omegas! Take their heads; the spirits must die."

Augie had already noticed that two of the demons were not the normal warrior demons they had been fighting. These auras were brighter, larger and the toothy jaws were much bigger. Her ancient memory recognized these demons as a second-order or arch-demon wielding more power and commanding over many other demons. These demons would not be afraid of being shot; they would attack. At the very least, these arch-demons would sacrifice the human host to survive so they could move into another host, and more importantly warn their leader. The demons had to die or they would soon escape to notify the other Omegas. This of course would make their secret known, and they would have to fight them again in another human body.

As she watched, her fears were realized. All the demons broke ranks and crashed into and past the guards to reach the other directors. Some shots were fired, but the arch-demons' auras, the ghoulish jaw, fought on, one grabbing the head of the Coast Guard Director of Intelligence and ripping it off. The arch-demon occupying the President was trying desperately to reach the Vice President, as the twins materialized. When the demons saw the golden auras appear, they bellowed in instant rage and turned and scrambled to reach the twins, but the huge golden hands of the gorillas ignored the ghoulish auras and locked unmercifully on to the human heads. Heads went flying, all of them, across the conference room to wetly splat against the walls and fall to the floor in a now very quiet room. The entire room watched the withering red auras slowly evaporate into nothingness.

Director Shepard said, "That, Vice Admiral, is the enemy, and that's the only way they can be killed! And, these young people that just saved you are some of the good guys. Are you ready to hear our story now?"

143

The Director of Navy Intelligence said with some enthusiasm, "Yes, I believe we are!"

Director Shepard directed one of his agents to get the demon human bodies removed and deploy "Plan Bravo". When asked what was "Plan Bravo", he said, "We are about to have a terrorist attack, one that unfortunately kills our President, Attorney General, Director of Army Intelligence, Director of Coast Guard Intelligence, Assistant Director of Air Force Intelligence, and a visiting Assistant Chief of MI-5. This will also provide a good cover story for going into high security level alert for the military." He laughed at a question about the AG and said, "Didn't I mention that the AG is a demon?"

"Does this meet with everyone's approval? Does this meet with your approval President Loveland?"

The new president, having narrowly escaped death from the old president's arch-demon, was still in deep shock and just nodded somewhat enthusiastically.

As a form of dramatic emphasis, Augie teleported Jack and Jill back to her dais in full view of all the CIA's guests. They began to shimmer then vanished from their site and returned to Mount Olympus.

After all the bodies and heads were removed and some of the blood covered up, Director Shepard brought Mr. Henderson into the room and introduced him as liaison for the good guys, the Alphas, and encouraged them to use their glasses again to see what a good guy looked like. He again mounted the podium and continued, giving a detailed description of all that had happened over the last few day. Director Setliff and Jack Ward took the stage also and over the next few hours brought all the guest up to speed to that point. Few questions were asked, and really none were needed due to the abundant detail of the report.

Augie was impressed, but when the narrative continued, she was anxiously attentive. This was all new information.

Director Setliff took the podium and began, "Our FBI operation in Quantico has been successful in duplicating the technology of the sunglasses, which you now possess. Originally, we were told by the Alphas that they could not be replicated, but as many of you know, our technology in optics is exceptional. It was not easy, but we were finally successful, and we now have hundreds available for your individual agencies. Just remember the very existence of these glasses is beyond ultra-top-secret."

"At this point this is our only advantage. The Omegas do not know about the technology given to us by the Olympians. Our analysts believe that the Omegas will launch an attack on any organized resistance once they find out their secret is out, so we don't have much time. Our number one priority right now is operational control of the military. That is why you are here, and only you. The more agencies involved, the greater the risk that the secret will leak out. If it does, we will lose this war before we can begin fighting it."

"We have sent out demon purged FBI teams to identify the enemy and their locations. I am sorry to say that the Omegas are everywhere, but primarily in the government. Congress and the government bureaucracy looks like a sieve. We suspected so and we refused to let the Director of NSA contact the president, and we already knew that the Attorney General is a demon. Thankfully, we have, or will have after the terrorist attack, a clean president and NSA Director."

"Mr. President, I hope you understand that you can't go back to D.C. They will find a way to kill you. No, under the cover of the terrorist attack you will be transported to Camp David ... after we purge that facility. You will run the government from there and these directors will protect you by use of the military."

"The military hierarchy must be purged immediately or we stand to lose our country. Not only must we purge the enemy, but we must be prepared to complete a military coup. It may not be necessary as long as we can protect the president, but if he goes down, all branches of the military must act. The enemy will come after us. Imagine, assuming that you didn't know what you now know, that you received a direct order from the next president to launch a missile on Langley." He let that register in their minds then continued, "See what I mean?"

The Chief of Great Britain's MI-5 coughed for attention and said, "I can see the gravity of the situation here in the colonies, and I certainly appreciate being invited here, but why was MI-5 and Massad included in this exclusive USA high level meeting? I think we obviously have our own problems at home that we need to get to. By the way, can we have a supply of those glasses to take with us?"

146

Director Setliff said, "Of course, you will be given glasses. As to the reason you were invited: as our closest allies we feel comfortable with both countries knowing and using the discretion as is obviously required to maintain the secret of our only advantage. Another reason is that if the USA falls, at least someone can carry on the fight. These are all good reasons to invite you, but the real reason is that you were actually invited by the Olympians, as will become obvious during the remainder of this presentation."

He didn't wait for a response and launched into the second phase, "Our Behavioral Analysis Team has completed extensive interviews, mostly unproductive, of the captured demons , but we have managed to developed a profile to help identify them. We have also completed extensive blood and DNA analysis to further identify them. This has been much more helpful."

We have definitely isolated DNA characteristics common to all bodies inhabited by the demons. We believe these signatures represents DNA from the original Titan race. As we now know, the Titan spirit is immortal, unless killed in a manner as we have witnessed, and at the death of the host's body this spirit passes to another descendant of the race. We can now identify these descendants, and apparently the Omegas have this knowledge as well and have carefully picked descendants as recipients of the Titan Omega spirit."

We can say this with some confidence based upon the profile of the demons. When an Omega spirit transfers into a Titan descendant, it literally

147

takes over control of the human mind. The human mind retains its previous knowledge, but the Omega spirit controls it. The Omega spirit, for lack of a better words, is pure evil. It doesn't learn. It can only use the knowledge the human host contains and what it brought with it. Some of the demons, the warriors, we interrogated were simple-minded, almost zombie like, but they blindly follow the instruction of their Omega superior. We believe the level of intelligence is based upon the age at which the Titan spirit inhabited the body. For this reason we also believe that the descendants are chosen in advance after the human's accomplishments, probably even groomed and educated for a specific task. It is the only way to explain how the Attorney General and the President were inhabited by Omega. They would not be able to reach this high level while being inhabited by Omega."

"Now, Mossad specifically? The Olympians believe that the Omega spirits will be concentrated primarily in the Middle-Eastern countries, because that is where the original Titan race inhabited and where a large concentration exists today. Our analysis supports this assumption. We also believe that the centuries of conflict between Arabs and Jews is a direct result of the conflict between Alphas and Omegas. Do you see where the assumption is going?"

"We believe, in some unexplainable way, that Alphas DNA may exist in Israel and they may have been protected from extermination by this ancient conflict. We believe this is also the reason why much of the Arab world wants to exterminate the Jewish race ... to kill the Alphas. By contrast, we do not believe many, if any, Alpha descendants have survived in the Middle-East outside of Israel. Their and our hope is that you may find some existing Alphas there, and they want to save them."

The Director of Mossad said, "Let me put the question bluntly. You suspect that the Jewish race has protected the Titan descendants capable of harboring the Alpha spirits? You also believe this is what has caused the hate between our races for centuries?"

Director Setliff said, "That is putting it bluntly, but yes, we suspect this may be the case. For whatever reason, we believe Israel harbors a higher percentage of the Titan Alpha Spirit DNA, and the Jewish race also seems to share many common traits. It is unclear whether that is by DNA or the fact that Israel, as a nation, has prevented their beheading. Either way it could explain the irrational hatred and certainly support the belief that Alphas may exist in Israel. The only DNA we have to compare is Mr. Henderson's here, and there are some similarities in his DNA and some sample records of Jewish DNA. There is a possibility, but we need to do more comparison and research. I have already talked to Mr. Henderson and we have requested blood specimens from the other Alphas and the Olympians."

"At any rate, this is why you have been invited. At the very least, Israel is a major ally and should have a chance to survive."

"Now, MI-5? Again, England is our greatest ally, and we always fight together. America wants to help you if we can. Another reason is that MI-5 operates the best intelligence agency in all of

Europe, and the Olympians believe there may be other Alphas in northern Europe, and they hope you will help them find them."

"Sadly, far too few Alphas have survived. So far they can almost be counted on both hands. This is far too few to face the demon armies that must exist. As you have seen, they have powers, and the Alphas will be overwhelmed in this coming war. If they lose, we all lose. We must help them save our world from this evil."

"One other thing I need to inform this group about. We have located the Omega headquarters in the US. We traced the employment records of many of the Omega warriors killed. They were all employed through various companies in the Rose Building in New York. We sent agents there to observe, and they report that at least half the people coming and going there are demons."

"If the Rose complex is behind this, we all know the vast wealth and power it wields all over the world; it's unequaled. Even without an evil army, that alone is intimidating.

"This is all we have to report at this time. Time is short and all of you here have to convince your commands. We are here if you need us. Take a case of glasses with you when you leave, and good luck."

Augie was still trying to process all the information she had heard when Ralph's mind transmitted to her, "Augie, are you still observing? Can you see me?"

Augie was still hovering above the room, but her mind was elsewhere. She refocused and observed Ralph standing by the podium with a doctor and bag full of equipment, "Yes, I see you."

Ralph said, "Can you bring me and Dr. Weiss there? I would rather talk in person."

The four Dark Angels pulled them toward the mist, and they soon stood before them on her enlarged dais. Mr. Henderson had little experience with teleporting, certainly Dr. Weiss had not teleported before, and they both looked a little pale as they stumbled out of the mist.

Augie said, "The FBI has been busy."

Ralph said, "They have been very busy, more than you know. That's what I wanted to tell you. They can now identify Titan descendants by DNA, but they believe there is a difference in those descendants. One DNA strain that accepts Omega and a different strain that they think accepts Alpha. I remember a discussion about the gods' bodies eventually dying and needing the Dark Angels to save them when they transfer into a Titan descendant's body. Well, Dr. Weiss believes she can identify the DNA and find an appropriate body host for the gods to transfer into. This way we can eliminate random chance and control when and where the transfer takes place. No danger or risk that Omega will find them before we do. It sounds like an excellent plan to me."

"It will take more research to accomplish, however. Dr. Weiss wants to draw blood from the other Alphas and the gods to do the research."

Augie was amazed at the plan and quickly agreed, offering up her arm to the Dr., and the other Dark Angels, having followed the conversation,

151

quickly lined up behind her. They all wanted to help the gods.

After all the blood was drawn, labeled and stored, they all proceeded to the Assembly area. Everyone seemed excited that the gods would like the plan, but the gods had obviously been watching and had their own plan.

Zeus said, "We cannot allow you to take our DNA. Thank you for the plan, though, but you still don't understand our existence and the nature of the problem. At all cost, we must not allow pure immortal Titan essence, you call it DNA, to again exist on Earth. This is what caused the problem in the beginning, and it has taken many centuries and hundreds of generations of humans to alter the Titan DNA into Alpha and Omega. This is the current war. If our pure Titan DNA were exposed to Earth again, the corruption could start anew. So, there will be no DNA samples from the gods."

"Now, having explained this, we do welcome the research on the Alphas' DNA, since we have already purged our spirits of Omega, the Alpha descendants will be the human host we would transfer into. We agree that your research could increase our chances of survival when we finely do expire, which is approaching far too rapidly."

What the gods had to say made sense. They always did, and there certainly was no objection from Dr. Weiss. Actually, although well-schooled with many accolades in her field, the Dr. appeared greatly intimidated by the Olympian gods and stood rigid and wide-eyed. Although pleased with their acceptance in part of her plan, she remained uncomfortable and was anxious to leave.

Dr. Weiss was visibly relieved when the group went back to Augie's quarters and anxious to get back to Langley to continue her DNA research, but just as they entered the mist, Heracles stopped them.

Heracles said, "Dr. Weiss, are you finished with the Omegas detained at Langley?"

Startled, she nodded and said, "Well, yes. I have their DNA on file now, and I believe the interrogations are finished."

"Good," said Heracles, "Then some of us need to go with you to make sure the demons are killed. They said they were planning a terrorist attack to cover the death of the other demons, and they also said the Attorney General was going to die in the same attack. I wouldn't put it past them to just lock him in the car and let the explosion kill him. Personally, I don't want to have to fight any of the demons again. I would rather make sure the Omega dies the first time."

"Woooa!" said Augie, "I'm not sure how many the four of us can teleport.

"It's Okay." said Heracles, "Just teleport Asteria and I. The demons don't have weapons anyway. Plus, Asteria and I are anxious to try out our aura images as weapons." At the surprised look he continued, "Yep, the twins taught us how to use them."

Augie wasn't terribly worried for Heracles and Asteria in battle, even against those odds, and as Heracles had said, they have no weapons. So, she said nothing as they joined Mr. Henderson and Dr. Weiss in the mist, but she was resolved to watch the battle in the mist and maybe the resistance from the CIA Director.

The main meeting had broken up, but many had remained in the room continuing other related discussions. As the group appeared in the conference room, silence fell heavy on those still assembled, and all eyes turned to stare in awe at Heracles and Asteria. This caused Augie to take a second look at the two warriors, and she too was impressed. The two warriors stood like golden statues standing silently in their black gothic attire. The impressive muscles on both stood out like coiled springs ready to strike. They really were intimidating, and if possible, they appeared even larger than she remembered, towering over any in the room.

The spell of silence was broken when Heracles demanded, "Show us the demons! We came to destroy them!" After a moment of continued silence Heracles said, "Now!"

At that, the entire room seemed to jump into action, some slipping on their glasses to see what the others seemed to be staring at, while others simply moved to give the warriors more room.

Director Shepard seemed to make a quick decision and said, "Certainly, follow me." The Dark Angels fell in behind him, and the entire group fell in behind them, obviously intent on watching.

When the Dark Angels entered the detention area, bellows and growls erupted from both sides. The demons and arch-demons went instantly berserk, clawing through the bars to reach the Alphas.

Heracles said, "Open the doors."

154

Director Shepard said, "We can't just let you go in there and kill them. That wouldn't exactly be legal."

"Legal?" said Asteria, "You better wake up! They are killing us and anyone that gets in their way, and they mean to control and enslave you. Don't you understand that?"

What happened next astounded Augie. Heracles said, "Enough talking!" Angry, he then turned toward the bars and simply passed through them as if his body was as transparent as his aura. The bars passed through his body as if there were no resistance. His body flowed around them and back together on the other side of the bar, and he was inside the cage. Asteria passed through the bars right behind him. They stood together side by side and took the demons as they came.

Augie and all in the room watched in shocked silence as the two warriors took the attacking demons apart. Heracles' golden bull aura solidified and swung from side to side catching the demons with the horns. The horns mutilated the charging bodies, dismembering heads and slinging them to either side, while Asteria's solid golden panther emitted a piercing scream and attacked, sinking its fangs deep in the necks of the bodies, then used the huge, clawed paws to finish ripping the heads off. Asteria took extra pleasure mutilating the arch-demon, the Attorney General, because of its larger aura, which actually managed to sink it teeth into the panther and draw blood. But, the arch demon was no match at all to the fury of the screeching and raging panther.

155

After the last demon charged and died, the warriors waded through the pile of bodies to observe that all had a red aura withering in death. Satisfied, they walked back through the bars to join the others, still staring in shocked disbelief.

Heracles said, "It was self-defense. You did see them attack us, right? That's legal! Bring us home, Augie."

As soon as they solidified within the mist, Athena said, "How did you do that, just walk through bars?"

Heracles said, "I really don't know. I just needed to get inside the bars, and my Alpha spirit made it happen."

Asteria said, "I just saw him do it and followed. It's almost like our spirit can do what needs to be done."

The arch-demon's bite on the panther seemed to transfer to Asteria's shoulder, and seeing the blood trickle down Asteria's back, Helen immediately rose from her throne and began healing her. It was not a serious wound and Helen's application of the blue glow corrected it quickly.

# Chapter 11
## The Olympians' Metamorphosis

Mojo had been so confident that his ancient plan was finally coming to fruition that he could not accept the set-backs. His organization and armies had destroyed many Alphas, but far too many had survived and came together, and he had lost many warriors to these cursed Alphas. They should have been easy to destroy, because there weren't that many, but the cursed Alphas had joined together and were remembering their powers and fighting back. Without doubt, the Olympian gods were helping and protecting them. They must all be destroyed.

He had armies of warriors and had spent centuries trying to identify the Titan descendants. Those descendants that served his purpose as hosts or future hosts for the developing Omega spirits were cultured, educated, and promoted or elected to positions of power, and they were put in high places to be occupied later. He had been extremely successful in placing his Omegas in high places. He now controlled many nations through Omega dictators or through control of their militaries.

Those descendants that might host the Alphas were systematically killed, because he had no way to know if they hosted a dormant Alpha spirit already, plus they needed to be eliminated for their potential future use. Those Alpha strain descendants were difficult to find until Earth science discovered DNA. Since the beginning of this science, he had medical teams researching

DNA to identify those descendants. By the mid-1990s most major countries had begun some form of criminal DNA databases, which he quickly tapped into and combined with his own personal database. Since then, his plan had progressed rapidly.

Armed with this information he was able to pick and choose those descendants he wanted to host an Omega spirit and was able to plant his minions deep within world governments. He was not yet within complete world control, but he did have substantial influence and limited operational control in western countries. In contrast, Mojo had virtually absolute control over the middle-east countries of the Arab League. Israel was the only exception of that region of the world. They had resisted his efforts to exterminate the Alpha DNA descendants, especially since many were Jewish or living in Israel and their moral aversion to beheading and mutilation from suicide bombers. The Israelis considered it terrorism, mostly because the majority of his demon army were Arab and the ancient enemy, but they would lose this battle soon.

Mojo's current focus was in the U.S.. The damn organized Alphas were destroying far too many of his warriors. They had evaded his traps. They had destroyed his armies sent after them, but he had mobilized his armies to spot them and discover where they were hiding. Once he located them he would simply bomb them out, even if he had to launch military attacks at them. Of course the Alpha spirits might survive, but it would wreck their current team and what organization and current powers they have remembered and developed. It would give his armies a new chance to catch and kill them as the spirit occupied a new body. It should be easy.

One thing that puzzled him was the possible involvement of the FBI. They had set up a "Hot Line" to identify, as they called it, glowing people. What did they know? Initially, he welcomed the idea, since he had demons on the inside of most police organization, including the FBI. They had intercepted many calls and his armies quickly found and destroyed the emerging Alphas, but that had suddenly stopped. His agents on the inside had been silent since. He suspected the agents had been discovered, but he didn't understand how. He sent his arch-demon, the Attorney General in to find out more, but he hadn't reported back either. There were rumors of terrorist activity and communication blackouts, but he had not authorized any terrorist activity or attacks.

As he sat pondering these things, one of his assistants came bursting into his office announcing a reported terrorist attack and explosion of an official U. S. government motorcade. He quickly turned his TV on to CNN, but it didn't matter what channel it was on. All channels were breaking in with emergency interruptions to announce the attack, which apparently was successful in killing the President, Attorney General, and several Directors of Military Intelligence, including an Assistant Chief of MI-5. He was instantly angry.

This was devastating! It destroyed years of planning and manipulation. Most of these people were Omegas and highly placed Omegas at that. Two of them were commanders, arch-demons, and

159

in an explosion of this type causing mutilation, the Omega spirit could have been and probably were killed, too, lost to him. Mojo bellowed out, "Find out who did this! I did not authorize any terrorist attack. Someone is going to die for this." His assistant fled from the room and from Mojo's legendary anger.

***

Seve said, "You know, I think the Olympian magic is NOT in the mist. I think the magic is not really magic at all. I think our Titan spirits are creating what we need or think about. Of course, it looks like magic to humans, but it's not. It's our power, and I think we can use it better."

"I think you are right," said Athena, "I think the power is within us, but have you noticed the gods lately? They don't seem to have much power left. They don't look right, almost transparent. They're getting lethargic and seem to be slowly fading away. The last time I spoke to my father, Zeus, it was like he didn't even hear me. I don't think they are searching for Alphas. I don't think they are doing anything. We need to do something."

Augie said, "Jessica, do you really remember being Athena and daughter of Zeus?"

Athena said, "Yes, I do remember ... somewhat. It seems right to call Zeus father, and I am Athena, but I am also Jessica, too. I remember how it was before. I guess that is why I notice the change in the gods so much. It is not like the way I remember them. Before, they had unimaginable powers and were always energetic and constantly fornicating with each other and humans in the world."

Laughing, Asteria said, "Do you remember that, too?"

Athena burst out laughing and said, "None of your damned business!" At that everyone laughed. "But seriously, they did say they purged their Omega spirit, and in a pure blood Titan they need both sides to make a whole, where we have the human spirit to make us whole. They also said they intend to transfer into an Alpha spirit descendant. I guess that will change them substantially and make them more like us."

"Well, what I am trying to say is that we need to take over here at Mount Olympus, since they are beginning to fail, and they aren't taking care of business. We also need to find some Alpha descendant hosts for them, otherwise we will have to search for their reemerging spirits."

Little Sue said something startling, "Well, if we need to find Alphas, why don't we just tell the mist to take us to them? You know, like Heracles and Asteria needed to go through the bars, and it happened."

Silence filled Augie's quarters as each of them stood staring at each other. Augie said, "Out of the mouths of babes comes wisdom. Seve, let's find some Alphas!"

Before they could begin a search, Ralph spoke to her mind, "Can I return now? I have information you may be interested in that can't wait. Oh, and I have a guest, also"

***

"You want me to do ... what? Are you out of your frigging mind?" bellowed Admiral Bill Neece, completely out of character for him.

161

Jack already knew the Admiral was pissed at him, so he thought he would let him get the bellowing out of the way, and hit him right between the eyes with his request. He had sent cleared FBI Agents to his home in Florida with orders to deliver him to the CIA at Langley, and that alone had the Admiral upset. He was not used to being summoned by FBI armed agents, especially in his retirement. Jack hadn't bothered to tell him that it was President Loveland's idea, well, him and Director Shepard.

Jack remembered the conversation vividly. He had been researching the military data base for Alpha descendants, and up pops Admiral Neece. By far the four star Admiral was the highest ranked Alpha descendant he had found. Amazing, since he had only found a handful. He took the information to CIA Director Shepard.

Director Shepard said, "You have got to be kidding me. I know him. We have worked together. He is a Navy Seal, tough as nails, and as far as I know, the only Seal to get that high in rank. Admiral Neece was head of the U. S. Special Operation Command for all branches of services, but I think he recently retired. The military forces you to retire after forty years ... damn shame. He was good."

"This is good news for our side. Stick around, Jack; I need to report this to the president."

"The president said, "Damn, I know Bill well: tough SOB, Annapolis grad, decorated ... Silver Star I think. Hell, he has been fighting these bastards for years and didn't even know it. Gentlemen, this is who we need commanding the military, especially if

162

he is an Alpha, also. You need to go get him before the Omega realize their mistake and kill him.

Jack said, "Admiral Neece, I know you're upset; I would be too, but I think you will agree it was necessary after you hear what we have to tell you. After we brief you the president wants to talk to you." Admiral Neece's anger was slowly replaced by curiosity, and after the lengthy and detailed presentation and a look through the sunglasses at Ralph Henderson, the anger returned with a completely different target.

***

"Of course," said Augie in response to Ralph's request to return with a guest, and the mist began to shimmer. As they solidified in the mist Augie quickly identified Ralph's guest. It was a full Navy Admiral with four gleaming gold stars and two very wide brown eyes.

Ralph said, "First, let me introduce Admiral Neece. The reason I brought him will become apparent soon, but let me give you a quick run-down of what has been happening below. The most important fact is that all the military branches are fully allied, and purging of all the headquarters is currently underway. Camp David has been secured and all the Navy and Marine Corp and Secret Service personnel at that location are cleared, and the president is running the government from the secure underground bunker there. The president has declared a state of war to exists. He hasn't named the enemy, just that the U.S. is in a state of war against whoever killed the president and the others. He declared martial law administrated by the military, which he now firmly controls. I can't tell you how close this was to being lost completely, and none understand this more than the military. Of course, few others even know the situation. We believe the secret of the glasses remains just that, a secret. All branches have exercised a total blackout on communication ahead of any security sweeps, and all demons found have been escorted to Langley under heavy security."

"The FBI has been researching the DNA databases, but unfortunately, most are criminal databases, and I told them that was unsuitable for finding an Alpha DNA host. But, we have a great database for military and intelligence agencies."

"This brings us back to Admiral Neece. The Admiral here is the highest ranking Alpha DNA descendant we have found. He fully understands the gravity of the situation, and he is willing to host an Alpha spirit. He says it will give us the best of both worlds, and everyone on their end agrees. It would also give the Olympians some control of our military, also. If the Olympians agree, the president will declare Admiral Neece the Chairman of the Joint Chiefs and put him in full operational control of all branches of the military."

"One other thing before we get side-tracked. Massad contacted Director Shepard and informed him that they have an Alpha in custody. They're sorry, but they didn't know the difference at the time. This Alpha had killed fellow soldiers and they captured him and have kept him in lockup. Apparently, the soldiers were Omegas, but this was before our last meeting. They want someone to come get him. Since they didn't understand, they haven't treated him very nicely. Honestly, after what their agents observed, I think they are afraid to open his cell door."

"Massad also reports that they have a fairly large collection of Omegas they have purged from their government, bureaucracy and military. I already told them how to kill them, but I think they remain a little squeamish. I think they will kill them alright, but I'm concerned they won't do it right to kill the Omega spirit. I think a team will have to go there."

Augie was quick to say, "Seve, can you and Sue find the Alpha in Israel? Damn, we need more Alphas on the dais. Helen, can you help on the dais? Twins, standby in case you are also needed. Heracles, Athena and Asteria, I think you are all we can send. Athena can control time if that is needed. I will stay to deal with the Olympians." No one challenged her instructions or authority. They trusted her completely.

Seve announced, "We have found the Alpha, and it wasn't that hard. The mist found him immediately like I thought."

By the time the three warriors entered the mist they were already shimmering and quickly winked out.

\*\*\*

Eli Joseph, at nineteen years old, was in his second year of the mandatory three year military service with the Israeli Defense Force. Mandatory service in the IDF applied to both males and females, so it didn't feel much different than being promoted to the next grade in school. All those you grew up with now trained and fought alongside you. Virtually every Israeli citizen was trained to fight when they turned eighteen, but when you live every day under threat of attack and annihilation, it's just the way it has to be.

Eli fit in well and had adjusted to life in the military, but all that suddenly changed in one eventful day. He was stationed at Camp Filon in the Golan Heights, and as usual, they were on a training exercise field. It was the day the sunspot activity began, changing the normal yellow/orange sunlight to yellow/blue. The pain built up in his head during that day until it overwhelmed him. He didn't know how long he was out, but he woke up in the base hospital with his head packed with ice. The nurse said he had had a heat stroke, but he was doing better.

He stayed in the hospital for two more days, then was released to return to his company. As he walked back toward his barracks across the open parade ground, he was charged by three screaming soldiers. They came running around the corner of a building directly toward him. Eli saw them coming, but what he noticed more distinctly were the red glows emanating from them. The glows had form and looked like ... hell, he didn't know what, something ghoulish and ugly for sure. Their intense hate bombarded him long before they reached him, and clashed with his own rage boiling up inside him. Eli didn't know where his intense rage was coming from. The three berserk soldiers were wielding and waving machetes and obviously intended to kill him. Why? He had no idea, but he had no intentions of being killed, even welcomed the opportunity to fight them.

It seemed to be taking them a long time to reach him, then he noticed why. They were moving slower than normal, but he didn't have time to analyze why. He attacked them. He had no weapon, but the rage inside him spurred him into action. The first soldier swung, but Eli easily sidestepped him and twisted the machete from his grasp. Now armed, he commenced his own brutal attack, chopping off arms, slashing throats, stomping and kicking. The three died quickly, and he stood over them watching the red glows snap at him and drift away.

Eli was still standing there with the bloody machete as the military police pulled up. They roughly subdued him, cuffed him and hauled him off to a prison cell. He kept trying to tell them exactly what happened, but they seemed to believe he was off the deep end. Guards then transported him to another detention area, and then the fun really began ... for them that is. He was tortured for answers he did not have. They kept asking him to name the others in his cell, where they were located, who did he report and answer to, etc. After a while he just quit talking at all, and they eventually stopped asking.

Eli lost track of time, but the sleep deprivation was part of the torture, but sometime later, probably days, a group came to just look at him. They passed a pair of glasses around as each stared at him. They mentioned a golden aura around him in the shape of an ancient dragon of lore, and they called him an Alpha, whatever that was. His keepers kept trying to talk to him, but he was done talking. They also talked about other Alphas coming to get him.

***

Once the Alpha team was gone, Augie quickly saw them form again in the mist in Israel, where they materialized outside Massad's detention cages. There was some initial surprise from the guards and administrative personnel when they suddenly appeared, but they were all wearing the special glasses and seemed to relax once they identified them. They were obviously expecting them, just not the method of transportation. Once the initial tension was over, Augie relaxed as well.

Sensing a compelling urge for speed and seeing no conflict in Israel, Augie swiftly said, "Seve, call me in your mind if anything goes wrong. I will hear you. Now, Mr. Henderson, Admiral, you too twins, come with me to the Assembly area. She wasn't quite sure why she called the twins, but it seemed right."

As they entered the Assembly area, Augie was shocked at what she saw. The gods were slumped in their thrones, hardly even raising their heads, and their bodies were definitely now transparent, like they were in the process of dissipating.

Zeus barely whispered, "Our time has ended, and we are fading. Sorry, we are out of time. You Alphas will have to take over."

"Oh, no you don't!" Augie yelled, "We need you, and we have brought Admiral Neece to host one of you. The Admiral is an Alpha DNA descendant, and we have found others. I can get some more here quickly, or you can transfer to some of us. You said Titan spirits can join in a single host. Let's do it!"

Poseidon had perked up when she mentioned Admiral, and now he said, "A man of the sea? I like that. I will accept his offer and make the transfer and give you what energy I still have so some of you can last a little longer."

Zeus was silent for a time then said, "Very well. Augie, maybe this will work, but hurry with your hosts."

Augie ran to an empty throne and spoke to Jack Ward's phone. When Jack answered she interrupted his greeting, "Jack I need addresses or locations for willing, well, willing or not, Alpha DNA hosts like the Admiral. I need male and female Alpha DNA descendants. Hurry Jack, please."

As she was speaking she noticed Poseidon transforming what was left of his essence into a golden aura of a large eight-armed octopus. After the aura was formed there remained no evidence of the body Poseidon once had. The aura drifted over to the Admiral and settled down over a very nervous Admiral. As the aura engulfed the Admiral it immediately grew brighter, as if it was plugged into a new charged battery.

After a few moment the Admiral smiled hugely and said, "Well, I'm still Admiral Neece, but I am also Poseidon; we are now one, and we are Alpha."

Augie said, "I'm pretty old, but I can host one of you for the short time I have remaining. You can always transfer to a younger host later."

As weak as Zeus was, he still managed a laugh, then said, "You still don't understand your new existence. Once we energized your Alpha spirit you and your body are now immortal and can manipulate matter. You can be as old or as young as you want to be."

Apollo looked at his sister, Artemis, then they looked at each other and nodded. Apollo said, "Artemis and I will join with Jack and Jill. It seems right, since we are all twins, and we love their auras already."

It sounded somewhat presumptuous to imply the twins had no choice, but in truth, none of the humans had ever had a choice since the beginning, but the twins weren't resisting. They too looked at each other and shrugged.

Apollo and Artemis transformed into golden clouds that then floated towards Jack and Jill to hover over them. The clouds gently encompassed the two youth, and immediately the gorilla auras flared brighter. Augie also noticed the gorilla faces took on some of the features of the Olympians, more than just a little, and almost simultaneously Jack and Jill began to smile. Their bodies also appeared to age to full maturity and the faces seemed to merge together . Apparently the joining was not unpleasant at all. She also noticed that the Admiral seemed to be at peace with Poseidon.

When Augie turned back to the gods, she instantly noticed Zeus, Aphrodite, Hermes and Hera all in transition to auras. When there was nothing left of those gods but the golden cloud, they began to float toward their chosen targets. Aphrodite and Hermes floated off toward Augie's quarters, and they could only be heading toward little Sue and Seve. Zeus went straight toward Mr. Henderson and settled over him. That left Hera, and she came directly for Augie.

170

Augie would rather have chosen another; she wasn't even sure she liked Hera, but she had volunteered. No matter now, it was too late, as Hera's aura settled over her. Augie felt the warmth of Hera's essence flood her as it filled her body and mind, and suddenly she saw both lives and remembered both lives, one ancient and long lived, the other seemed short in comparison, but they flowed together and she became someone new. They would not be in competition with each other; they were one. She felt the power renewing and growing within her. It was incredible.

Augie also realized why Hera had chosen her. There was great respect. Hera had relished in Augie's obstinate attitude toward Zeus, and how she had stood up to him, maybe she even envied her. Hera respected that, that and the way Augie had led and directed the Alphas. Augie also saw that Zeus was extremely powerful but needed to keep his feet grounded in reality. Together Hera and Augie would make a good team, and Zeus would have his hands full.

Hera's aura had had no shape, like the twins, Hera's aura had taken the shape of a cloud and joined with hers. This pleased Augie, because she secretly liked her golden bear aura. She called it her grisly, and that made her a mama grisly. Yes, this was going to work out well.

Augie's focused attention turned to Mr. Henderson and immediately burst out laughing, and she wasn't sure if it was Hera's or her humor that was triggered. The first thing she noticed was that Mr. Henderson had immediately dropped about forty years, yet maintained the white hair and beard.

171

The attire also conformed to what Zeus had warn. It was so like Zeus, the egotistical bastard, to have things his way, but it all seemed to fit them both. Zeus had maintained Mr. Henderson's highly dignified and appropriate aura of a magnificent male lion, but he had added lightning bolts in its paws. That in itself wasn't all that unusual, knowing Zeus, but the second addition just struck her as hilarious. Zeus had added a golden jeweled crown to Mr. Henderson's head, like the one he always wore. So, actually, it wasn't so strange for Zeus, but it was funny.

Augie couldn't resist, "Mr. Henderson, how do you feel?"

He smiled and said in a somewhat deeper and authoritative voice, "Hummm, we feel great, actually. We think this will work out well.

Poseidon interrupted and said, "This is interesting, but you know that there is a lot to be done as Chief of Staff, and I better get started." Those that could, immediately took their seats on their thrones, while the Admiral took his place in the mist and began to shimmer.

Augie suddenly remembered the deployed warrior team and sent her thoughts, "Seve, is everything going well there?"

"Oh, yeah, all is going well. This is a cool way to talk. Oh, we are going to use Hermes as our name."

Augie transmitted, "I think you three might want to come over to the main Assembly area and join the others."

"Yes, that makes sense. We'll be right over."

***

172

Athena thought after they materialized within the Massad detention facilities that they could have planned a little better, or at least called ahead. The guards were startled, and she was about to adjust time, if that was possible from a remote location, to keep them from getting shot when the Director of Massad announced all was well. The Dark Angels were obviously expected, and none but an Alpha would materialize out of thin air. Well, they did say come and get the Alpha.

Athena immediately saw the captive Alpha and heard him as well. The Alpha was pissed and screaming at his captors, but he stopped when he saw them. Their golden auras caught his attention, and he said in Hebrew, "What's happening here?" She didn't know how, but she understood Hebrew. It must have come with the spirit, because she, according to some, barely spoke English.

Athena said, "Speak English!" She apparently would have understood him, but she wasn't sure if the others in her team would, and she was pretty sure this Alpha did speak English, since almost every other country outside of the US spoke multiple languages, and English was usually the second language of choice.

"Yeah, fine, what's going on," he said, "Who are you guys?"

Athena said, "I don't know how much you know about what's going on, but we are Alpha spirits just like you. They didn't know who you are. Now they do, and ask us to come get you, so don't retaliate and come with us. OK? You will be safe, and we will explain everything to you."

"Yes! Hell yes, get me the hell out of here."

173

He had stepped forward into the light as they spoke, and she had gotten a much better look at him. He was a large man, not as large as Heracles, but of substantial size. He appeared to be in his early twenties. His face was ruggedly handsome with a dark complexion, but his deep blue eyes grabbed her attention. They were penetrating and angry. His aura radiated brilliantly in the form of an ancient golden dragon of legend. The long neck of the dragon curved high holding blazing eyes and large jaws snapping the air. If this aura solidified it would be extremely dangerous to an enemy.

Athena said, "I love your golden Aura."

"I have been locked up here," Eli loudly said, "I haven't had a chance to see it."

Athena briefly described it for him, which seemed to please him.

"Director, you can let him loose now," said Athena, "and show us to the Omegas. We can work off the anger."

The Director looked dubious, but he ordered the cage opened, then they all stood back behind the Alphas. The Alpha walked out slowly, still visibly angry but marginally in control of himself. He ignored the Massad guards, all of the Massad personnel, actually, and continued over to the other Alphas and said, "My name is Eli, and I suspect that I will now learn whom I have become and why."

They all made their individual introductions and bombarded him with information, of which he was getting about half, but he was learning quickly.

The Director broke into their discussion to say, "Follow me, and I will take you to the Omega

174

compound. Am I to understand you wish to kill them all?"

Athena, having learned from the last engagement said, "No, we intend to defend ourselves."

It was a fairly long walk which took them outside to a heavily fenced area housing about sixty, now bellowing, demons. As soon as the demons saw the golden auras the demons went crazy trying to get to them. It startled the guards and one of them shot into the compound.

Heracles bellowed, "No! Don't shoot. It will only kill the body and the demon spirit will get away and enter another body."

"I didn't know that," said Eli.

"There is a lot you need to learn," said Asteria, "But we will teach you," as she tossed him one of her swords. "Chop the human head off the Omega's body and it will kill the demon." Eli grinned and nodded.

The fence rattled, buckled and crashed to the ground from the weight of the demons' human bodies, and they charged. The Dark Angels waved the guards back and stood to defend themselves. At least they didn't have to walk through the fence this time.

Athena couldn't fight and generate the time energy to her full level, so as it was in her first battles, she just slowed them down. The mob of demons had only their rage as weapons. Still, they continued in massive force, but in slow motion; while the Dark Angels attacked.

Heracles had his double bladed axe churning over his head, while his glowing horns waved at

175

closer range, and heads were flying through the air. Asteria's sword took many more heads, while the vicious claws of her panther worked their devastation. Eli was slower to fall into sync. At first he looked a little frightened, but he fought bravely and well. During a lull, while changing position away from the increasing pile of dead bodies and slippery blood, he noticed the others using their aura, and began experimenting. Soon his golden dragon flared to life, and before long the claws and huge jaws went to work.

Athena loved using her super speed and agility with her sword; it was fun. But, she was anxious to let her aura work as well. She missed the last battle using nothing but the auras and was eager to see what hers would do. When it began, she was shocked. She expected the claws of her giant owl to become weapons, which they did, but she did not expect to see the long, thick wings to flare out and sweep. The energy in the tip of the wings acted like giant swords, slicing through muscle and bone. It was awesome and frighteningly devastating to the rushing demons.

All too soon it was over. All the possessed humans were dead or dying, the small battlefield withered with evaporating red demons, and the Massad personnel and guards, even the Director, stood in stunned silence, eyes and jaws wide open.

As the Dark Angels prepared to leave, Asteria said, "Next time electrify the fence, or better yet, kill them the right way. I'm surprised they didn't force you to kill them so the spirit could escape and possess others."

\*\*\*

176

When the Alpha team returned to Mount Olympus, everything had changed. The first obvious change was that the whole team of Alphas was now positioned at the main Assembly dais. Secondly, many of the gods were missing, not all, but most, and they had been replaced by Alphas ... changed Alphas. The third and probably most significant change was the fact that Ralph Henderson sat in the center throne formally occupied by Zeus and was apparently now directing this new Assembly. Upon closer examination, Athena noticed the prominent addition of a crown on the head of a much younger Mr. Henderson's golden lion aura. This in itself spoke volumes about what had happened, and the physical locations of the Alphas added to the story.

Augie had changed, too. She too was also much younger and now dressed in a white wrap very much like Hera had dressed. Although changed, there was no doubt it was Augie. Other changes were less obvious. Seve, Sue and the twins looked older, but still dressed in black leather as they had emulated from the other Dark Angles. Karrie, however, seemed completely unchanged, much to Heracles' obvious pleasure.

"Welcome back Alphas. You did a great job. We watched in the mist." Augie said, but at the sharp look she received from Mr. Henderson, she continued, "And Zeus, you can cut that crap out right now. These are my team as well." She sensed Hera smiling at her response.

Athena looked back and forth between the two sitting side by side and said, "Thanks Augie," in a somewhat questioning tone.

177

Augie tried to imagine how her looks must have changed to Athena, but so far she hadn't considered the changes. As with Mr. Henderson, she probably appeared younger, and by looking at her white sleeves, she must assume they (Augie/Hera) had adopted Hera's white fine linen attire. That wasn't so bad; Hera had looked stunning in it. She must still be recognizable as Augie for Athena to address her as Augie, even if the address had a question mark.

Augie said, "As you may have guessed already, many of us have joined, and we," pointing to herself indicating plural, "go by Hera now, and they," pointing at Mr. Henderson, "are Zeus. You will quickly discover the other changes. The gods were fading out and we had to make some sudden changes, and we aren't finished."

Asteria said, "Do you need us to join with anyone?"

Zeus answered, "Thank you for the offer, but not right now. The changes we have made were necessary, sudden and made sense. We are trying not to combine with you existing warriors. Olympus needs warriors, as many as we can get. Apollo and Artemis are already warriors and they have strengthened the young twins. Hermes and Aphrodite have strengthened the young Seve and Sue. They are all now competent and mature Alpha warriors. Those of us that are now Alphas are not confined to Mount Olympus and can join the rest of you in battles on Earth. Augie/Hera has a plan for the other gods that remain in danger of dissolving away without the rest of you getting involved directly."

178

"Before we continue let me welcome our newest recruit, and you truly are welcome. We witnessed you battle with the other angels, and you are indeed a welcome addition to our group. The others will educate you with what you need to know and answer any additional questions you may have. I do not recognize your Alpha spirit, but you obviously have a very strong Alpha spirit. Until we identify your dominant Titan ancestor we will continue to address you by your human name, Eli. Again, welcome."

# Chapter 12
## The World Tunes In

As the startled team of Warriors found seats provided by the mist outside the control dais ring, Jack Ward's voice came out of the mist, "Augie, are you there?"

"Yes, we are here,"

"I'm sure there are many more Alpha DNA descendants, but I have only been able to gather four, two men and two women, mostly military. How many more will you need?"

Augie said, "That will be perfect. Where are they?"

"Here in my office," Jack said.

"Thanks. Have them wait, and we will get them."

The joined new Assembly sped through space to look down into Jack Wards office, but there were only three people other than Jack in his office. Augie said, "Where is the fourth?"

Jack said, "I'm the fourth. Would you believe it, I'm an Alpha DNA descendant?"

She didn't wait, and the Assembly quickly seized them. They didn't even have time to be startled until they materialized within the mist.

The mist cleared leaving the three military personnel still standing at attention, although they didn't seem quite as rigid on weakened legs. Jack had seen it all before, but the others began to look around the new surroundings in disbelief. There was a female Army Colonel in dress uniform, a female Air Force Major, Jack Ward and a grisly Marine Corps Master Sergeant.

The usually quiet Ares said to no one in particular, "Oh, I want to join with the warrior," pointing at the grisly Marine Corps Master Sergeant.

Hera/Augie looked at Zeus and said, "May I speak for the Assembly?" Receiving a nod from Zeus she said, "We have little time. Do you all understand this is for life?"

Zeus added, "An immortal life, however." This last comment seemed to raise some eyebrows from the humans. She hadn't realized the Alphas' new life had become immortal until after she joined with Hera and fully understood the situation better, so the volunteers obviously wouldn't know how their lives would change. The gods had mentioned that they could alter matter, and their physical appearance was just another form of matter. So, the merger went far beyond just immortal; it allowed physical appearance, even physical age alternations as well. Life would definitely be interesting for all of them.

Jack spoke for all of them and said, "Yes, none of us have families, we're all near retirement, and we are at war, a war at this point we could easily lose. We all have discussed the situation at length and freely volunteer. As you can see from Master Sergeant Reynolds' campaign ribbons, he has been in every major campaign the Marine Corp has been involved in over the last thirty years. As Ares indicated, Master Sergeant is a warrior and wants to continue to be. It would be hard to exclude him. Major Watkins and Colonel Blevins, while not quite as enthusiastic as the Master Sergeant, are true patriots and want to serve in whatever capacity they can.

It was already too late to back out, as Ares, Hephaestus, Hestia, and Demeter had already begun to fade into nebulous golden clouds. All the auras remained uncommitted in form as they floated toward their targets. Ares was the first aura to settle down over the Master Sergeant, and once their personalities joined, the aura slowly formed into a large wolverine, vicious and snarling. Its long sharp claws clicked together, looking for a target. This seemed fitting, since Ares has long been considered fearless and vicious in war. Apparently, so was the Master Sergeant, and his grisly face split with a huge grin at the aura. This would be a superior warrior without doubt, and now in a human body, could leave Mount Olympus for battle.

The next aura to settle over the Army Colonel was Demeter. When they were joined their golden aura began to form in the shape of Pegasus, the black, winged horse. The horse's head stared and turned from side to side, the front legs and hooves pawed the air, and the wings flared. To be honest, the aura wasn't all that intimidating, but Demeter "mother of the house", and Mount Olympus seemed to be the house. This also made sense. Who better to monitor and manipulate the dais but a goddess supplemented with a vast amount of earth knowledge with the colonel.

Hestia was the next aura to settle over the Air Force Major. After a few moments the joint aura became shocking. A golden flame sprang to life within the aura and seemed to accent the shoulders and head of the major. This too made sense once

182

you thought about it. Hestia was considered "goddess of the hearth" and her symbol was eternal flames. She would not be a warrior; she would be another guardian of Mount Olympus and the dais, and truly they needed some like her.

Hephaestus' aura was the last to settle over Jack Ward, and the image that formed was a black and golden tiger. The huge, clawed paws were very intimidating. This new Alpha would become a formidable warrior, although would continue to work with the FBI.

The four new Alphas began smiling and milling around. Evidently none of the new partners had a problem with the new togetherness. Actually, why should they? It wasn't like the two personalities were competing; they were now new joined but a single personality.

Augie did notice, however, that the military personnel maintained their impressive uniforms, and in Jack's case, the customary suit. It made sense, since Jack would be rejoining the FBI. She had to assume that the gods liked the uniforms and the symbolism of Earth's elite military.

The learning curve began as they all took their places at the dais. There was no quicker way to learn and mingle with the other minds, and no spoken communications was required.

*** 

Poseidon had changed. He thought differently. Well, that wasn't entirely true. He was still Poseidon, but he was more. The Admiral had a dynamic persona, hell, so did he. Now together they were more, which pleased him greatly. They were in a new environment, an environment in which the ancient memories did them little good. Poseidon still had his memories and his powers. He could communicate telepathically with the other gods, but they would now be in the Admiral's world. He hadn't been on Earth in thousands of years. He had monitored much, but this was the Admiral's world and his knowledge would have to lead hear, but he could support him. The world knew him by Admiral, so Admiral Neece would be their name, at least on the Earth.

The new and improved Admiral was teleported back to Langley, where he immediately took Director Shepard's office and contacted the president at Camp David. He said, "Sir, it is done."

"Fantastic!" said the president, "I have already declared Martial Law. Now, I will declare military control of the government and assign you to the position of Chairman of the Joint Chiefs and give you temporary control of the United States answering only to me for the duration of this emergency. Go clean them out, Admiral, and Admiral," after a long pause he continued, "Don't get killed."

He chuckled and said, "Aye, aye, Sir."

The Admiral took Director Shepard's desk and chair and said, "Status report."

"Director Shepard immediately recognized that he and the CIA would fall under the authority of the Admiral and have a major role in the upcoming campaign. He held nothing back. "The FBI headquarters and at Quantico and the CIA here at Langley have been cleared of all Omegas. I believe you are already aware of these facts."

"Camp David has been swept, and the president is secure there. The top brass of Operational Control and Command, those controlling the troops, of all branches have been cleared, and they have isolated themselves from the chain of command. The political secretaries are going crazy, but the Commands are with us, and they have begun to work down the chain, but those at the highest level at the Pentagon remain unknown. The Marine Corps base at Quantico is currently in the process of being cleared, and most of that has been accomplished."

"The FBI has manufactured thousands of the aura viewing sunglasses. They're going everywhere, but still controlled by the intelligence community. They have even been able to modify the electronics and lenses for video cameras and satellite equipment to see the auras, but we have not cleared the NSA yet, so we haven't deployed them."

"We have captured hundreds of Omegas and secreted them here to Langley, since we are one of the only secure locations. They are kept within electrified fences."

The Admiral interrupted saying, "Director, the president will soon be announcing my appointment as Chairman of the Joint Chiefs with total temporary overall Command of this emergency. Since this is your facility, you will be my temporary Chief of Staff to speak with my authority."

"The first thing I want you to do is dispatch Omega purged troops from Quantico to Camp David with orders to protect the president at all cost. Also dispatch cleared troops from Quantico to secure Langley. I know you have good security

185

here, but you made a mistake bringing the Omegas here and keeping them in the open. We will become a target once they fully discover we know about them. Now we must protect ourselves." Poseidon immediately notified Zeus about the Omega prisoners.

"I want an umbrella of fighters in the air above both places, add the Pentagon to that list. I don't want a mosquito to get through, and Director, make sure those pilots have been cleared."

"Shall I include Washington in that list?" asked Director Shepard.

The Admiral barked, "I would have told you if I did. Washington is not yet secure and not likely to be any time soon."

"Now, I want new rules of engagement only for the cleared troops. None of these Omegas are to be shot. If they need to be subdued use tasers. I want the security troops to be issued the glasses, tasers and swords, and if you don't have enough swords, use machetes. Officers are to wear their swords at all times. If they are engaged, hear me good now, the Omegas are to be behead."

"Dispatch secure orders to Quantico, and only to Quantico, to prepare for a full lockdown of the Pentagon on my order. They are to use overwhelming force to effect the lockdown. Even so, the secret will probably get out. It's getting too big to control the secret much longer anyway."

"Now, the last thing. Call an emergency meeting here for all the Joint Chiefs, Secretary of Defense, and the Secretaries of the military branches. Let's get those levels cleared so we can move forward."

Zeus and Ralph had internally compromised on the name. They called themselves Zeus Henderson formally, but among the familiars it was still Zeus, since Zeus was the known leader of the gods, the one with the power. Ralph was in agreement, and thankfully Ralph accepted Zeus' customary dress. Actually, he kind of liked the white kilt, wide golden belt, and white fine linen blouse, but the crown was a little much.

Zeus addressed the Assembly and said, "Ralph has brought a vast amount of information concerning the modern world, and we believe we need to go public. I think we need to bring a reputable NY Times reporter to Mount Olympus, someone that is respected and will be believed. We can let him or her take pictures and hear the entire story about what's going on in the world and the battle that is being waged against humans. The story is too big to keep hidden, and it is bound to get out. It's better if we control the outflow of information, and get the public on our side. I've communicated with Poseidon, and he is not anxious for the world to find out, but he agrees that the truth is better coming from us. Who knows? Maybe we will become the heroes."

Hera said, "That's a good idea, but maybe we should also recruit reporters from the news channels. They could set up a studio here and work up a documentary, even follow some of our exploits through the dais."

"Excellent idea!" Zeus said, "let's make it happen.

187

Hera led the Assembly through the dais and the combined mind sped toward its destination, the New York Times building, then into the hustle-bustle inside. They floated through the building and found a reporter with a private office. She assumed this was a good indication of a prestigious position. The name on the office door said, Janice Metz, and she sat behind her desk working on her laptop. They waited and watched her work until she got a call. She quickly picked up the laptop, camera and pad and headed off down the hall. They followed her into a conference room filled with other reporters. She was greeted by the others and while she was in full attention of the others, the Olympians snatched her away. She was still screaming as she materialized within the mist.

The scream cut off immediately when she witnessed the Assembly and crowd of apparently strange people, and she starred in awe. Were they that strange? she wondered. Hera looked around at those she was with, and had to admit, yes, they looked strange. Zeus, of course looked frightening, as always, and she had to laugh at her own joke. Hestia was sitting there in her Colonials uniform, but all the Dark Angels were wearing the goth black leather, all but her. She was dressed in the white fine linen robes. Even the twins, hosting gods, were decked out in black leather. Helen had somehow created, through her individual dais, black leather apparel for all of them, and Eli, not to be out done, had already adopted black leather with large silver spikes. Seve and Sue, as young as they were, must have influenced their new god partners, Aphrodite and Hermes, wore black leather. It looked like a goth convention. On top of all that, spikes, swords and axes adorned the lot, even Helen. No wonder Janice starred; they were not only strange but also a scary lot.

Hera said, "Janice, please don't be concerned. We mean you no harm. We brought you here to give you a story, and it no doubt will earn you a Pulitzer Prize in journalism. If you like, we can send you back and get another reporter."

Janice swallowed her fear and said, "That won't be necessary. I would simply die of curiosity if I didn't write what I know is going to be one hell of a story."

"Very well," said Hera, "Please step out of the mist and join us here. We have another task to preform before we start."

Janice did as she was asked, although cautiously, but quickly turned her attention back to the dais and the image developing in the mist to watch in amazement as the Assembly's perspective sped off through space back to New York City. Soon they were hovering over a popular editorial host. For effect they jointly decided to take him in the middle of his program, while millions were watching. Sean Brannon was in the middle of a dialogue when he began shimmering, then winked out in front of a startled crew, but their shock increased as they too began to shimmer, along with their equipment. They all appeared in the mist soon after, and they were a very shaken group.

Hera quickly said, "We mean you no harm. Please be calm. We brought you here to record a story and interview whomever you wish. We think you will like the story."

189

Sean was quick to recover and said, "Well, it's looking interesting so far, but you pulled me right off the stage in the middle of airtime. That will take some explaining."

"We wanted the world to see, to get its attention. Besides, I think you will agree it's worth it," Hera said, "Now, please step out of the mist and join Janice Metz up here. I think you might know her from the New York Times."

Sean, the boom technician, two camera men, and producer all came up out of the mist with all the equipment, but the producer said, "We don't have all the equipment we need, besides, I don't even see a power outlet."

Zeus spoke for the first time saying, "Don't worry. It will all work and you will be able to transmit your video directly to your studio. You won't understand how, so don't ask. You won't need electricity either; it will work. Hermes, give Sean and Janice a phone so they could contact their offices. Also give them a pair of the glasses to see auras."

In a small portion in the upper mist the Assembly activated what appeared to be a viewing screen presenting the Fox News Channel. The video had no borders and looked nothing like the screen on a TV. It was far better quality and three dimensional. They brought it up because Fox News was covering the disappearance of Sean, showing him shimmering and fading out in the studio. The video was running a loop of the sequence and talking heads and scientist were speculating on what had happened, none of them correct, however.

Sean and Janice quickly took the phones and called their offices, and could be heard talking fast. Almost as quickly, Fox News broke into their transmission and reported that Sean was calling in, and immediately put him on the air. "This is Sean Brannon and I am reporting from ... hell, I don't know where, but I was ... teleported here along with Janice Metz from the New York Times. We are alright and unharmed."

"It doesn't look like Earth. It looks like ... believe it or not, Mount Olympus, and the person in charge calls himself Zeus. Go figure! We are told that we were brought here to report on a story so fantastic it will be hard to believe. I suppose that is why we were taken so publicly." During Sean's rambling he slipped on his glasses, and yelled, "Holly Shit! Oh, sorry, but you're not going to believe this. Just wait until you see. We are told that we will be able to transmit video soon, so stay tuned to Fox News."

Hephaestus/Jack Ward was also on his phone talking to Director Setliff letting him know to keep tuned to Fox News. In keeping with the new attempt to notify the public, he suggested that the FBI contact Fox News and help them modify their equipment in order to view and transmit the invisible auras.

Director Setliff said, "I think we better do more than that. We will need to send over teams to purge both the New York Times and Fox News and protect them. They might come under attack from internal sabotage and from outside. The Omegas will definitely not want this story to get out to the general public."

191

"Since we are doing them a big favor, saving them, I also think both of those companies will give us free advertisement to sell these glasses to the public at large. We couldn't keep up with the demand, so I have already established a manufacture to make them. I like this going public. It makes it hard to silence us."

Zeus gave Sean and his crew time to get set up then began. Initially, it was a one-way presentation, and the influence of Ralph's professor and public speaking skills made the presentation both interesting and factual and not so much as a king talking down to his subjects. Zeus led Janice and Sean through the ancient history of the Titan race and how the Titans and humans mingled and mixed, how the genetics mixed and the problems it caused, how the Omegas manifested themselves in the truly evil men/women of history, how the Titans recently activated the dormant Alpha spirits to fight the Omegas, and he explained the recent mutilation killings of the Alphas and Omegas as they fought back. Janice and Sean both asked probing questions that he tried to answer as best he could. He held nothing back. Well, he did withhold sensitive security information but very little.

Sean and Janice then began interviewing each member and recorded their stories. Seve's emotional description of how his father had pushed him out the door to save him and forfeited his life in the process generated sympathy in all. Helen/Karrie's description of her families brutal death and the trap to kill the Alphas added to the picture, but the reporters showed much interest in Athena's story of Jessica and how she saved so many Alphas and killed so many Omegas. They easily accepted the fact that Heracles had killed many Omegas protecting himself and others, but Aphrodite embellished little Sue's story of being kidnaped by Omegas on a school yard and saved from death by the Alphas. Augie noticed that for this interview Sue's appearance had reverted to the little girl she had been. This would be a television special all by itself. The reporters also focused on the Japanese twins and the Israeli, Eli. At Zeus' insistence the reporters agreed to hold the story of Jack Ward's involvement. Zeus felt much of that information might be too sensitive and revealing to the enemy. There was enough detail in all the stories that could easily be verified, each becoming a human interest story likely to generate a following of fans.

***

The reports were coming in to Mojo from his many agents, and they were disturbing. Somehow the military in the U.S. were purging his agents. They knew! Only the damn Alphas or the gods knew the truth and what to look for. Damn them! He hadn't taken over control yet. Now it was too late. He had waited too long to take over, in the U. S. anyway.

The military had been busy and they had kept their knowledge secret. Maintaining secrecy from his agents and him was a major accomplishment, since he had agents positioned everywhere. It started with the FBI and CIA. Once those agencies went into lockdown, none of his agents emerged from those organizations. Many of the military bases followed suit, and he must presume they had also been purged.

Now the Pentagon was in complete lockdown and communication blackout, and those valuable agents within would be lost. Agents outside notified him that they had witnessed several battalions of Marines storm the Pentagon and surround it in a full lockdown. Several of the reports mentioned special glasses being used by elite military units that apparently allowed the wearer to see the demon auras. This is how they knew, and that knowledge could only have come from the Olympians. Damn them again!

Mojo's rage boiled. He 'should have seen it coming when his arch-demons had been killed in that phony terrorist attack, because he did not order such an attack. There were no rogue terrorist cells. He controlled them all. The spirits hadn't resurfaced either, which was a sure indication that the spirits had also died. He should have realized it when the new president, replacing his agent, declared martial law. That had been a totally unexpected move, but he was slow to identify the source. No, his nemesis, Zeus had to be involved.

Declaring Martial Law effectively took the control out of his hands. It bypassed the Congress, which he owned, and he had lost contact with those in immediate control of the military. He must assume his agents had also been purged, and without them he couldn't launch assaults on the CIA and FBI, at least not from the U.S. military.

He seriously considered having Russia launch missiles to destroy the CIA and the FBI headquarters, but that would provide a target and invoke automatic retaliation and war, which would result in losing thousands of Omegas in Russia. No, he needed those agents and an operational government in Russia to control. He would not provide a target for America, which is why he used terrorist attacks to mask the identity of the offenders. If America couldn't identify an offending country, they wouldn't be able to declare war.

Unfortunately, the Olympians and Alphas, with the help of the CIA and FBI, had done irreparable damage to his operational control in America, maybe too much. His control was the weakest here. That is why he put an office in New York, so he could implement his control. Most of the rest of the world was his already. Maybe a war and mutual destruction of America and Russia is what he should do, but he would need time to evacuate all his agents, and he didn't have the time. The other reason for keeping the U.S. intact was that America was wealthy and he wanted it and the people to enslave. But, right now his demons were in danger, and he needed to evacuate them for use in a counterattack.

If the military was capturing his Omegas, they had to be putting them somewhere. He didn't think they would kill them, but if the Alphas found them gathered in numbers they would kill them and the spirit. He had to find out where his captured agents were, but none of his agents had heard anything, and none of his agents that would know had come out after a lockdown on a facility or military base.

He contacted his agents in NSA to search for them through the satellites, and luckily they still responded. By all reports there were hundreds of Omegas not reporting. They would almost certainly have to be imprisoned in the open, and if they were being held in the open, the NSA would find them.

It didn't take the NSA long to locate the imprisoned Omegas. The CIA was guarding them in a secluded fenced in area of the woods within the security of Langley. According to the report, there were hundreds of them captured. He didn't care about the human bodies, but he needed those Titan spirits. He could find more of the Omega DNA descendant bodies to use, plenty more; but if the spirits were killed, there would never be a way to replace them. He had to protect the spirits. This was his priority.

Mojo's issued new orders to all his agents: they were ordered to kill themselves if captured. That would be the escape for the spirit. He also called up two cells to attack the compound at Langley. The spirits would be released. The last order was also a general order to all cells in the U.S. authorizing Jehad. All cells were released to exercise each cell's prearranged attack. Mojo wanted to cause as much disruption as he could before the enemy could get more organized. This would keep them busy and off of him and buy him the time he needed.

# Chapter 13
# Battles Rage

The reporters weren't about to leave and took quarters at Mount Olympus so they could continue to gathered historical information and fodder for many future stories that would last for months, but action continued in the present, especially when Poseidon/Admiral Neece's image blossomed in the mist and said, "Assembly, the Omegas have begun terrorist attacks all over the U.S., and they are killing many people. It is full jehad. They have also discovered the location of the captured Omegas and have already made an attempt to kill them to free the spirits."

"Two crop dusting planes tried to overfly ... " he caught himself before he disclosed the exact location ... "the area, but we were prepared and shot them down. When we inspected the wreckage, we discovered poison gas. It would have killed many other civilians as well. We need to take them out before the Omegas can free those spirits to take over other humans."

Zeus said, "Indeed we do. Dark Angel warriors gather in the mist." The Dark Angels immediately jumped into the mist, but as Hera began to go, Zeus said, "No, Hera, you must stay. We need you here to help with the dais. Seve, you and Sue stay as well. Neither of you are quite ready, and we need you on the dais." Seve and Sue both looked disappointed, but complied with the instruction, taking their place at the dais.

"But they need me to seize time," Hera argued.

"No, my son, Apollo, has the power, and Athena can help. Eli also has limited power, but Helen has the strongest ability. She just doesn't know it yet."

Apollo had already sided up to Helen, explaining the power and how to use it. The two of them were ignoring the others, as Helen listened intently and nodded. It was quite obvious Apollo wanted to engage in the battle and not stand in the rear. He had been confined to Mount Olympus far too long and wanted battle.

Zeus looked to the newly rejuvenated Jack Ward with his vicious golden tiger aura standing to the side and said, "Jack Ward, if you like, you may also take your place with the warriors for this battle before rejoining the FBI."

Jack, although being totally engaged in the problem so far with the FBI, was initially shocked, then petrified at the thought of actually being a warrior and going into battle. He had never been in a battle of this nature before and assumed that when Zeus said warriors enter the dais, he meant the others. After the joining he had maintained the look of an older man, thinking it would be more acceptable at the FBI, but his old body felt young and very strong, ready for battle. Now he thought, Why not? I ... we ARE a warrior now. He then smiled and joined the other warriors still dressed in a business suit, getting a few slaps on the back as he did.

Sean said, "Will we be able to watch the battle here in the mist?" He didn't wait for an answer, rushing one of his cameras to focus on the dais, while positioning himself to narrate the battle.

This would be the largest battle yet, but this would also be the largest group of Dark Angel warriors to deploy. So what if the odds were twenty to one.

The Assembly teleported the nine Dark Angels to the least populated end of the enclosed compound, and the reaction was immediate. The Omegas bellowed their outrage and charged toward them screeching, armed with nothing more than their uncontrollable rage and their flailing hands.

As was customary for the warriors' defense, Heracles stood in the middle flanked by Athena and Asteria. Helen stood to the rear with Apollo. Apollo was coaching her, and her arms were lifted high, as if reaching for the sky. Helen was finely successful and seized time and held it firm, allowing it to flow slowly. The charging horde of demons immediately slowed and appeared to be moving in a pool of molasses. She grinned wide with her accomplishment, and Apollo, satisfied, nodded and then took his place beside his Japanese twin, Artemis, in the front line. Ares joined in the Master Sergeant's body stood separated, apparently not needing or wanting assistance, but Eli took a place in the line next to Ares and waited. Jack was pleased that Hephaestus knew what to do, having borrowed one of Asteria's swords. They took a position at the end of the line beside Athena and watched the horde come.

Watching the varied expressions of hate on the demons slowly approaching left little doubt of their malicious intentions. The Dark Angles launched into the demons when they came within range, their rage equally in evidence. Although the angels had weapons, it was mostly their auras that fought. Heracles' horns cut a wide, vicious path; Athena's wings spun like the blades of a helicopter and sliced off heads as if they were wheat to be harvested; Asteria's angry panther hissed, sliced, and ripped heads; and the twin gorillas popped off heads and limbs as fast as they came into reach. It was like picking apples from a tree and even sounded like it, but that wasn't fast enough. The twins left the defense line and ran into the horde avoiding the slow moving snapping demon jaws, rolling to reach more of the enemy. Jack Ward's golden, black-striped tiger raged and mutilated and ripped demons and bodies. To be new at battle, he was a natural, but of course the experience in battle came from his Olympian partner. Eli's golden dragon jaws and claws mangled any demon within reach, but the Assembly and onlookers of the mist stared in awe at the avenging Ares.

Ares lived up to his ancient reputation as a savage warrior, and the grisly Marine likely shared his savagery, because the wolverine aura viciously sliced through meat and bone with the long, razor sharp claws, totally mangling the demon's bodies. Heads and limbs flew, and what happened to be left was raked with long knives whirling in the muscular arms of the Marine.

The mutilated bodies piled up and the blood and gore became difficult for the footing, and several of the Dark Angels slipped and fell in the goo, but always the adjacent angel covered the fallen. As a line, they began slowly walking forward into the crowd dispensing their ancient vengeance, but there were still hundreds of them.

It took some time to take the destruction through the entire complex before they began looking around for a new enemy target and finding none. The battle was finely over and the compound was full of withering and dying demons spirits. The Dark Angles were now covered completely in the red blood and gore of the destroyed demon army, hardly recognizable except for their bright auras.

Asteria had taken a nasty stab to her right leg when she had slipped and fallen earlier. The demons were slow, but still very dangerous. Once the battle was over, Helen went to her and applied her blue glowing, healing hands to the gash. After Asteria was healed, Helen went through the other Dark Angels healing a few minor cuts they had suffered.

Sean had intended to narrate the battle as it played out, but he failed terribly. Viewing from the dais' perspective the seizure of time did not affect him, and he and the other viewers saw the carnage in real time, complete even to viewing the auras unaided. At the end he was still on camera starring silently in shocked awe toward the mist. He was not speaking at all and his mouth was wide open, and Janice looked much the same.

Zeus broke the shocked silence when he said, "The battle is over."

Sean visibly jumped and screamed at Zeus, "You just mutilated hundreds of humans!"

Calmly, Zeus said, "No! We just killed hundreds of attacking Titan Omega spirits occupying bodies that were no longer human. They were what many today would call zombies. They looked and acted like humans, but their minds were pure evil and no longer theirs. They belonged to my brother, Hades, who controlled them. They are also the suicide bomber bodies that are out there today blowing themselves up to kill humans, destroy property, or create chaos. Also remember that we prevented the loss of hundreds of other humans, because had we not killed the Titan Omega spirits in the manner we did, they would have stolen the lives of other humans and jehad would have continued. Do you understand?"

Sean hung his head in thought, but soon focused himself and looked at Zeus and said, "I'm sorry. Yes, I understand. I was just reacting to the carnage I witnessed, but I truly do understand." He had forgotten the camera was still recording and transmitting to the studio. The whole world had watched the battle and discussion.

The Dark Angels, having completed their task, returned to Mount Olympus. When they materialized within the mist their appearances were in stark contrast to what they looked like after the battle. On the battlefield the Dark Angels were covered from head to foot in blood and gore. When they reappeared they were clean and fresh, as if they had never been in battle.

Sean stared, seeing the contrast in appearance and said to no one in particular, "How can this be? They were covered in blood, but now they are fresh as daises."

It was Hephaestus/Jack that responded, "We control matter through our dais. We simply didn't return the mess matter. It would serve no purpose."

"By the way, Zeus, now that the battle is over and the team is back, I think now that I can do more good back at Langley."

"Yes," Zeus said, "Keep us in the loop."

*** 

After notifying Zeus the Admiral immediately went to the compound and witnessed the battle. It was an epic battle, and he was pleased to see the destruction of so many demons. His only regret was that he was unable to join the Olympian warriors, but his current position dictated that he lead and not participate as a warrior. But, it was just the beginning of the war, and his opportunity would come. Still, he watched his fellow Olympians fight with envy, especially Hephaestus and Jack Ward in his business suit, tie flopping, ripping into the demons.

It was now time to purge the Pentagon. Once Zeus notified him about going public he knew the secret advantage of the glasses would become common knowledge. Oh well, the secret was bound to leak out, still, it forced him to move on the Pentagon a little sooner than he wanted.

The Marines had positioned themselves around the Pentagon and sealed it off and cut or jammed all communications, and began sweeping through the many corridors and rooms searching for the Omega demons. There were many, and they were not being killed; they were being gathered in a detention area. Even though their new rules of engagement not only encouraged but directed the military combatants to behead them, they were reluctant to start. The Admiral knew he would have to go there.

The Pentagon would be his new headquarters, and since he now had a large staff of assistances and security guards, it was impractical to teleport. He made the decision to motorcade there with his entourage. He also told CIA Director Shepard, "Since I'm going to have to go to the Pentagon, you might as well move the meeting with the Joint Chiefs and secretaries of the military to the Pentagon.

He met with the CIA Director Shepard, the FBI Director Setliff and the newly returned now Olympian/Jack Ward to let them know his plans. Most here had witnessed the battle between the spirits and more specifically one of their own, Jack Ward. Jack was receiving more than his share of respectful stares, even awe, from his staff and colleagues.

Since both the FBI and the CIA were now purged, at least the major facilities, Director Setliff was returning to the FBI headquarters in D.C. to resume control of his operation. He would remain a part of the Admiral's staff, technically. This would prevent any bureaucracy from injecting itself between them. Director Shepard would continue as his Chief of Staff, for a while anyway, and Jack Ward would also remain in his staff. It made sense to have an Alpha watch his back, but now it was time to retake the military's headquarters at the Pentagon. The NSA Director Campbell was still unable to return to his organization, so the Admiral directed him to join his staff at the Pentagon; which pleased Director Campbell greatly. Now he could get seriously involved and maybe contribute to the cause.

The motorcade made quick time and the trip was uneventful right up until they got close to the Pentagon. They stalled in traffic caused by the lockdown. The internal security, police force, and Marines, already sanitized of demons, were desperately trying to clear and open the traffic for their entrance, but the sheer volume of vehicles in the traffic jam prevented them. As an alternate method of access, a detachment of Marines quickly approached on foot suggesting that they abandon their vehicles and allow them to escort the Admiral and his staff through the clutter of stalled vehicles back inside the secure area. The Admiral immediately agreed, and transmitted his intentions to Zeus.

The Admiral gave the order and they exited the motorcade and gathered inside the perimeter of Marines and began a long procession through the stalled vehicles. Unfortunately, due to the closeness of the cars, they had to spread out in a long line. They had traveled through most of them and were in sight of the secure area when he heard a shot ring out behind him. He quickly turned to see van doors flying open and demons leaping out. The doors blocked his security in the rear. A Marine blocked by one of the doors had fired a warning shot. Then he heard another gunshot and quickly turned to see the same action in front of him. He was blocked by more demons, and he and Jack were isolated. He yelled out, "Don't shoot them! Use your machetes." Four demons ran toward him swinging swords from the front, and he was obviously the target.

He didn't have time to teleport out or grab time, so he stood firm to face his ancient arch enemies, and he heard the roar of a tiger behind him and knew Jack was facing his own enemies. As they closed on the Admiral his octopus arms shot forward, two of them wrapping around the heads of the closest two demons. These massive arms quickly pulled, spinning the heads like a top. Two more octopus arms reached out to latch onto the demons' swords. Now armed with two swords, he used them to slice off the crushed heads. His eyes remained focused on the other two demons approaching. Other octopus arms snaked out to grab the feet of the approaching demons and yank them off their feet. With the two demons dangling upside down he used the swords to chop off their heads. The Admiral spun around to face the demons behind, but Jack was engaged and in his way. He sent octopus arms snaking down to grab some demon legs to pull them off balance. Jack's tiger had torn two demons apart and was moving on the other two, but the other two demons spun bottom side up and were dangling upside down. The demons were chopping at his octopus arms, but the swords sliced through only his aura without any damage. It was as if his image was only a cloud. Jack's tiger viciously clawed the upended demons apart. As he dropped the mutilated mass, Hephaestus's persona turned and said, "It was worth the wait in exile to have fun like this."

There were three other demons close, but the Marines had engaged them, and were following his new rules of engagement. They fought with their machetes and were chopping their heads off. It pleased him to see the withering and dying demon spirits.

They surveyed the area for other enemies. There were none close, but he could see a red demon aura escaping through the traffic. This was most unfortunate. He transmitted to Zeus, "Now Hades would know for sure he had been compromised. The secret is out."

Zeus said, "Yes, we watched in the dais and understand, but hopefully it is too late for him to stop us. Besides, I'm sure Hades has already heard. The TV is full of stories about us."

Marines came running, seemingly from every direction. They were still shocked from the ordeal, but Marines are trained to function, even in shock. The Admiral waved them back and said, "I'm not injured; I'm fine. Let's get behind the safety perimeter."

The Admiral was covered in blood from the battle and received many stares as he and his staff made it through the barricade to the building entrance to meet the gathered Joint Chiefs. As soon as he made it inside he stood to the side and barked, "Report." The other Admirals and Generals stumbled over each other to report, and he noticed that all of them wore the special sunglasses. Seeing his aura obviously added to their discomfort, but they reported.

The Marines and internal police had already made a preliminary sweep through the main building gathering and herding the Omegas into the central courtyard. They reported that some of the Omegas during the struggle had killed themselves and others had been shot.

The Admiral was instantly fuming and bellowed, "You let the Omega spirits escape? I ordered the Omegas to be beheaded! Hell, I just personally killed four of the bastards myself, and now they don't have heads."

The Marine General commanding the Quantico forces stepped forward, snapped to attention, saluted briskly, and said, "Sir, we are following the new rules of engagement, but some of the Omegas had some sort of suicide tooth they bit down on and they died immediately before we could get to them and kill the spirit. Once we saw what was happening I ordered my men to behead any of the Omegas that fell or resisted. Luckily, there were only a few like that and all the others are handcuffed."

The frustrated Admiral said, "So, General, what are we to do with them now? They are pure evil. They are not human, and if they win, you will be their slaves. They are zombies and servants to the Devil. Now we have to kill them with their hands tied? That goes against our humanity and training. Now I will have to bring in the Alphas to do your job. Is that fair to the Alphas? No, it is better to kill them initially. Kill them on sight! I don't care if they are the Secretary of Defense or one of the Joint Chiefs." He suspected that had been the case, since some of them were missing. They would have been arch-demons and were probably the ones that committed suicide. He continued, "Do you understand? Does everyone understand?" Only silence met his stare.

The Admiral transmitted to Zeus, "Will you filter all this blood off of me and Jack?"

Immediately he began to shimmer, and all the blood was gone. He now stood in front of them smartly in a crisp clean uniform and in total command.

The Admiral took off at a fast pace, heading directly through the complex and then out into the courtyard where the Omegas were kept. He didn't look back, because he knew they all followed. As soon as he was visible to the Omegas, bellows of instant rage emerged and echoed off the buildings. The Marines ran to build a line between the Admiral and the now charging Omegas. The Omega's rage provided the extra strength to break the tie-wraps binding them, and they began to help each other break free and charged, ignoring and roughly shoving the Marines on guard. The word had apparently already spread, because the Marine guards began slicing into the Omegas with their issued machetes, and the line of Marines met the charging Omegas. The Admiral refrained from seizing time, as it would have only served to slow all the humans, including the Marines.

Unfortunately, due to the sheer mass of Omegas, the enemy managed to overpower a few of the Marines caught in the sudden charge and took their machetes, so by the time they reached the line of Marines there were clashes of steel. No more Marines fell, however, and soon all the Omega demons lay screeching out their ancient evil souls. The Admiral believed there would be no more captured Omegas in the future.

The second sweep of the Pentagon only found a very few Omegas, who were immediately killed, so the Admiral allowed the Pentagon to resume full operation, although maintaining extremely heavy security.

A more detailed status report revealed that in fact, The Secretary of Defense, and all appointed civilian secretary posts of the various military branches had been Omegas, which was to be expected from the past Omega president. There, of course, were a few high ranking military that had also been compromised, including two of his joint chiefs. He immediately reported to the president, and the empty positions were being filled.

***

Sean Brannon had long since shaken his frozen shock of the battles, and narrated the entire scene for the viewing audience, which had now become most of the free world. Strangely, however, much of the world had quickly gone into television blackout soon after Sean had begun his transmissions.

The demand for more information was insatiable, and Sean had worked tirelessly to provide it. Luckily, the dais provided an almost endless supply. Even when nothing was happening in the dais Sean had continued to delve into individual human interest stories about the Dark Angels. One of his favorites was little Sue, and Sean, through the dais, had interviewed teachers from the school that had witnessed the kidnapping and the rescue. Sean had also interviewed her parents and let them communicate with her. It was heartbreaking to watch, and millions of viewers had watched. The parents were extremely happy that Sue had been saved and that she was now one of the world famous Dark Angels. Even the parents had become instant celebrities.

Seve was another success story. He was quickly becoming a folk hero in the Rio Grande Valley and a favorite son of Mexico. Any story about the young, always smiling, Mexican boy was sought after.

Sean had his studio research the history of all the Alphas and verified all their stories, backed up by investigating detectives and police reports, eyewitnesses, and family, where possible. All the Dark Angel warriors and the Olympians were now considered Earth's heroes, but the original four warriors, Athena, Asteria, Hercules and Helen, were universally accepted as the heart of the Dark Angel warriors. Augie's contributions were not forgotten either. Sean did an in-depth interview with Augie, and she had resumed her original age in looks. She said she didn't want the seniors to be left out.

Japan media was only too happy to provide information and interviews about the twins. The entire country was proud to have members in the Alpha Dark Angels representing Japan, but unfortunately, Israel was not helpful at all. They were possibly ashamed of their treatment of Eli, or they were in too much turmoil with their own internal battle for control.

Of course, all the other news media outlets were airing stories about the Olympian gods. Not having access to the Fox programming from Mount Olympus, they were carrying programs describing the gods of ancient Greek mythology. Suffice to say that the world was getting to know the Olympian gods.

# Chapter 14
## Don't Mess With A Redneck

An obviously excited Jack Ward/Hephaestus flashed into view in the dais and began talking immediately, "Augie, you aren't going to believe this shit! Oh, sorry about the protocol, but none of you are going to believe this shit!"

Laughing, Hera said, "Go ahead and tell us."

Jack continued, "You know those special sunglasses? We had a major manufacturer set up to mass produce them. Well, they have been in production night and day since the beginning and still can't keep up with the orders. Fox News even took them on as an advertiser. They are selling like crazy. You would expect many countries and law enforcement maybe, but average people are standing in line at Walmart to buy them. I'm telling you, the world is turning on the Omegas big time."

"Due to Sean's television specials, Dark Angel fan clubs have sprung up all over the country, especially among the young. Hell, little Seve is national hero in Mexico and all the Mexican communities. Japan is going nuts over the twins. They want them to come to Japan so they can put them in parades so the people can see and meet them. But, the Dark Angel fan clubs ... well, many of them are turning into vigilante groups seeking out Omegas and killing them, and they are killing them right to kill the spirits."

"This trend started in the southern states, but the movement is migrating north and west. Dark Angel Militia (DAM), they call themselves, in

Arizona are transgressing the law and sweeping the entire state and moving into California. They wear black sheets and hoods so they can't be identified and canvas towns for Omegas. You know what? Law enforcement isn't doing a thing about it. In one southern town the red-neck vigilantes stormed a district court and pulled the Omega judge right off the bench and dragged him into the town square and chopped off his head in front of a cheering audience."

"Most of the terrorist causing all the disruptions are Omegas, and the FBI has actually begun to feed the clubs information as to strongholds of Omegas. The Omegas are on the defensive now and moving underground. Well, all except those in congress. They are business as usual there. The Omegas do, however, still have control of some of the Secret Service, US Marshals and much of the head law enforcement in D.C. and many of the major cities, and they are protecting the Omegas there."

"Congress has passed laws to clamp down on the vigilant groups, but with 'Martial Law' declared and the military unwilling to enforce them, they are just spinning their wheels."

Zeus asked, "How is the rest of the world?"

"Well, England and most of Europe are fighting back for control, but their battle is hard. France is not doing well, and when we can, we may have to help them. Not much is coming out of Israel, but they mostly stay quiet, always have. Nothing is coming out of the Mid-East. They remain in a total blackout. All though agree that they are firmly in control by Omega. Asia remains mostly quiet. We don't believe Omega ever had much of a hold there.

213

Canada, Australia, Mexico and South America seem to be firmly imitating the actions of the United States, all except those with dictators, but we feel they will be ousted eventually when the glasses get distributed. The dictators are most likely Omegas. The leaders in the old Communist bloc countries are Omegas already or leaning toward the Omegas. We will have to watch out for them."

"India has surprised us. They found an Alpha there, and the entire nation has rallied to protect one of its own. The Alpha is an infant and is well protected. No Omega will even get close to it the ways it's protected. I suspect even we better leave it alone for right now. I am getting word of other infant Alphas, but I don't know a lot yet. It makes sense, only the very old or an infant would have been kept inside so long while the Omegas searched for them, but now the Omegas are moving underground."

Zeus said, "You are correct. It is hard to believe that shit, but I have learned one thing through thousands of years of observing humans; you can never understand how humans will react. So, I can believe this reaction."

"Thanks for the report and information, Mr. Ward. Now, based upon this information I think we need to expand the exposure. I think it is time to let the people see their Congress at work. What does the Assembly think?" Zeus surveyed the room and saw the understanding register on the faces and smiles spread around the room."

"What do you think, Sean?"

Sean was grinning when he said, "If you are talking about observing them through the dais, and they won't even know we are watching, I do think it is time to show the people."

The dais sprang into life as the Assembly sped through space then slowed as they entered the capital building and hovered in the air above Congress as they were in session. The camera focused on the dais and the images coming from inside. Sean couldn't help but spew out his disbelief. Among the congressmen at least sixty percent of them radiated out red demon auras. Even Sean couldn't believe it was that bad, but the Olympians had always known. Omegas' evil concentrated in seats of power, and Congress was the most powerful body in the United States. Now they just had to wait and see how the people would react.

To make matters worse, at least for Congress, they were debating a new law declaring assaults upon humans with auras, obviously Omega auras, as a "Hate Crime" and another law banning the use of the special sunglasses, calling it profiling. The debate was heated, but one the Omegas had the votes to win.

After hours of watching the Congressional carnival, Sean, normally reasonably neutral in his reporting, completely lost it. The cameras were rolling, but he forgot and began ranting, "Just look at these idiots. They think they own the world and can do anything. The pure audacity of their arrogance. No wonder their approval rating is in the toilet! Well, I guess maybe it's because most of them are Omegas." The camera operator caught Sean's attention and shocked him back to reality. He blushed and said, "Oh shit." Before he could begin his apologies to the viewing audience, Fox News broke in with a special alert broadcast from the president.

President Loveland's face suddenly filled the screen and began speaking, "Hello my fellow Americans and neighbors. I come to you tonight to make a special announcement concerning the grave situation we find ourselves in today causing me to declare 'Martial Law'. You would have to be living in a cave not to have heard the cause. These so called Omegas have been causing havoc throughout our country. They are killing innocent citizens (men, women and even children). They are also destroying property and attempting to destroy us from within. To protect our country and its citizens I have declared 'Martial Law' and put the military in charge of our safety. They are currently turning back the wave of Omegas destruction and many average citizens are helping, and you are welcome to join the fight. This is in fact your country, and we all must fight to protect it."

"Like many of you, I have been watching the actions of our apparently Omega controlled Congress. I, like most of you, am appalled by their actions. I am here to let the country know that until Congress is purged of the evil demons, as a legislative body they no longer speak for the citizens of this country in their efforts to protect Omegas. To aid in this I am declaring Congress insolvent during this period of 'Marshal Law'. Neither I nor the American citizens will tolerate any laws or attempts to defend these Omegas. I announce to America that my administration encourages the participation of our citizens in the nation's internal defense, and we will not prosecute Omega killings. If the citizens fight them, as they already are doing, they will not be punished. One caution, however, make sure they are Omegas. Any killing of unpossessed American citizens will be prosecuted to the fullest extent of the law. Having said that, let me now say that the citizens fought to build this country, and we will fight again to keep it. Let's take our country back!"

Sean actually cheered, "Way to go, President Loveland!"

***

For centuries everything went right for Mojo, but in the last few days everything has gone wrong. In fact it would be hard to say that anything has gone right at all since the Alphas awoke. But, he had no illusion of the cause. Yes, the Alphas had powers, but they were mostly still undiscovered. It was the Olympians that were the problem and threat, and it was the Olympians that would be the focus of his attack. Of course, if he had the opportunity to take out an Alpha, he would.

He had greatly underestimated Zeus. Going public was totally unexpected and quite effective in putting him on the defensive. Zeus had shown worldly knowledge that Mojo didn't think he had. Mojo had already written off America and turned his attention to Europe, Africa and Asia, where he initiated a complete information blackout and began his own public relationship programming. It would be easy to reinforce the hate that already existed for Israel and the West. His job was easier, because he already controlled the news released to the population.

217

His last function in America would be to free as many Omega spirits as possible. Unfortunately, most of the important ones, except for Congress, had been destroyed by the Alphas. But, the largest remaining concentration of Omegas was in Congress and D.C. That would be his target, and the easiest way would be fire, explosion, or gas would accomplish this.

The Olympians posed the hardest challenge, mainly because he didn't know where they were located. Hell, they could even be in another dimension for all he knew. But, he really didn't need to know where they were, because the Olympians knew where they were, and he had a plan. All the pieces were in place, and he was ready to make his move.

Some of the best visual engineers and technicians in the world were in England, and he had ordered them to build a holographic image projector to visualize a golden aura in the form of an eagle. They now reported that it was complete. Being a holographic image, it would be visible to all without the special glasses, but that shouldn't be a problem, since the Olympians saw auras anyway. Seeing the counterfeit, golden aura should easily trick them into believing it real.

His arch-demon in England had already assigned a fanatical (non-Omega) follower to the task. The fanatic human would wear the holographic projector and forty pounds of C-4 and metal fragments under his trench-coat. His arch-demon would call the FBI "Hot-Line" and report a golden aura. By the time the Olympians tuned in to search for the aura, the fanatic would appear to be chased by a team of demons. One of two things would then happen: the Alphas would teleport there to save him, or the Olympians would teleport the counterfeit Alpha directly to Mount Olympus. In the first case, the counterfeit suicide Alpha bomber would eventually, after the battle, be teleported with the Alphas back to Mount Olympus. The worst case scenario , should the counterfeit be discovered, he could destroy those Alphas. In either case, the odds of killing the Olympians was high. Any of the options would be good, but Mojo was anticipating a direct teleport to Mount Olympus. After the last near successful trap, the Olympians might be hesitant to teleport Alphas into another potential trap. He was also leaving nothing to chance, and if the fanatic backed out at the last minute, his arch-demon would trigger the time delayed detonation of the bomb to allow completion of the teleportation. Hopefully, the explosion would mutilate the Olympians enough to kill the spirit. If not, the Olympians would, at a minimum, be put out of commission. Even if he said so himself, it was a brilliant plan, and it would work.

***

"Admiral, something is troubling me." Jack Ward said after entering the Admiral's office.

"Hello, Jack. Talk to me," responded Admiral Neece.

"Well, I've been attempting to anticipate Hades' next move." Jack said, "Of course, any of us are in danger, but aside from that, what will he do? Going public has totally disrupted his plans here in the U.S, and he is on the defensive. I know he wants to kill Alphas, but he would also want to save

219

his Omegas, and they are being taken out at an alarming rate for him. We have killed many, and the vigilante groups across the country are also killing large number of them. If he hasn't already, he will be wanting to get the Omega spirits all out. I've been thinking that one the largest concentration of Omegas is in Congress. Neither we nor the vigilante groups have approached them yet, but I hear rumors about a million man march on Washington. Today, however, Congress remains untouched, and that's where I believe he will strike next. I really don't expect him to mass exodus the humans, because it would be far easier just to kill the humans and release the Omega spirits. I could be wrong, but I don't think so."

"Good thinking. I believe you are right." said Admiral Neece. "I'm assuming that you have compiled a list of all the Senators and Congressmen as to which ones are possessed or clear?" He waited to see Jack nod in the affirmative, then continued, "Send the list over to Camp David, and I will call the president and ask him to have his staff call the cleared ones and instruct them to go immediately to any military base and check in and remain there until notified. This will be a quick way to verify them and any staff they take with them through base security. It will also protect them from what action Hades might launch on Congress and get them out of the way for any action we might launch."

At the Admiral's summons, Director Shepard rushed into the Admiral's office. Admiral Neece said, "Director Shepard, please extend the air protection umbrella over the Capital, and dispatch troops to lock down the Capital building. This is as good a time as any to purge Congress. Oh, and director, make sure the troops have the proper gear for protection against any possible chemical or gas attack. Hopefully it won't come to that, but anything is possible."

"Yes, Sir," responded Director Shepard.

***

Jack Ward briefed the Assembly about the planned action against Congress, and they would definitely keep them under surveillance. His concerns made sense. Already they could see clear Senators and Congressmen exiting the facilities in much haste, and as expected, their staffs were leaving with them. It was a smart move to direct them to check in at a military base. By this time all the military security would have been purged and wearing the special sunglasses. So, any Omega aura, politician or staff, would be identified and immediately killed, assuming the military police were following their new rules of engagement.

The secondary benefit, and probably the most important, was that the pain in the ass politician would be out of the way. Now all they had to deal with was the Omega zombies, but if Jack was right and the Congress Omegas are the target, do they dare send the Dark Angels to deal with them? At least for the time being the military would soon have the Capital building in lockdown and not letting anyone in and only letting the normal humans out. As a result, the Omegas were being concentrated within the Capital building, and more appalling in that most of them were arch-demons.

These needed to be eliminated before they could repopulate Hades' ranks.

As they were considering the best course of action for Congress, Jack Ward reappeared in the mist to announce, "The FBI has received another call on our 'Hot Line' from England reporting a golden aura." He then gave them the address, but something in his demeanor was less than enthusiastic. "We got the call from someone at MI-5, but not the director. So, be careful. I'm not sure if I trust the report."

The Assembly was already seeking out the location in the mist, and they had no trouble in locating the Alpha. He wasn't at the address but running down a wide pedestrian sidewalk. He was easy to identify from his bright golden aura in the form of an eagle. About a block behind him were about twenty demons pursuing the Alpha. In an abundance of caution, they spread out their search to look for possible traps or ambush sites. They saw none.

Zeus asked, "Should we commit the Dark Angels? We could simply teleport the Alpha directly here.

Hera said, "Well, we have to save the Alpha, and it would be great to kill those Omegas."

Sue/Aphrodite said, "We like the eagle aura and want to save it and would love to kill more Omegas, also; but after the last time with their ambush attempt, I don't trust them. They have had time to plan something. Maybe we should just teleport the Alpha directly here."

There was a general agreement around the Assembly, and Zeus said, "Very well. We'll

222

teleport the Alpha and worry about the Omegas later."

In her life in the Air Force, Major Watkins/Hestia had served as an intelligence officer. She had been trained to notice things like body language, facial expressions, and to use her brain to analyze what her eyes saw. Something about the scene she was observing in the mist wasn't quite right, but she couldn't pinpoint exactly what it was. Suddenly it clicked, and she bellowed, "Wait! Don't teleport. It's a trick. That's not an Alpha; the aura isn't real."

The first thing she noticed out of place was the absence of pure hate and rage Hestia's memories informed her should be there in the Omegas in the presence of a real Alpha, but what really got her attention were the pedestrians. Their eyes cut up to stare at the aura. Normal humans should not be able to see the aura unaided, and none were wearing the glasses. If they saw the aura, the golden aura couldn't be real.

These thoughts transferred instantly to the others linked together in the dais, and it was Colonel Blevins/Demeter, analyzing with her anti-terrorist training and knowledge, that spoke first, quickly blurting out, "It's a suicide bomber!" After a pause and sudden internal revelation, she said, "We are the target."

Zeus was instantly pissed, but after a few seconds he slowly smiled and said, "Well, Hades wants us to teleport the false Alpha. So let's do so, just not teleport to where he had hoped."

The Assembly began smiling as they saw what Zeus had in mind. They watched the make-believe

Alpha begin to shimmer and pop out of existence then pop back into existence again a block away in the midst of the following Omegas. The Omegas were surprised, but they were not motivated by the rage of the Alpha. If there was ever any doubt, it vanished with their reaction. The suicide bomber apparently did not control the detonation, because the false Alpha stood in the middle of the group of Omegas and exploded. It was a large explosion, devastating and mutilating the Omegas, so much that only a few of the Omega spirits survived. The Assembly watched most of the spirits wither and die.

Seve said, "That was so cool." After a pause for thought, he continued, "Why can't we just teleport another bomb to where Hades is located and kill the leader?"

Zeus and the other gods appeared befuddled and looked at each in amazement then he said, "Young minds find simple solutions. Honestly, I'm not sure, but it's worth considering. Hades does have powers if he remembers them, but luckily for us, he forfeited many powers, including the power of the dais, when he purged his Alpha spirit. The power of the dais is an exclusive ability of the Alpha spirit, plus, the material of the dais originally came from Titan and isn't available on Earth. Still, these powers originate within the spirit and not the dais itself. So, he may still have powers, but they would be harder for him to evoke."

"Let's find out." Jack said, "The Omega headquarters is in the Rose building in New York. Hades should be there. Let's go look."

The mist cleared as they entered the Rose building, and apparently Jack was right. There were Omegas everywhere. All the security were Omegas and security was extremely heavy and got heavier the higher they went. By the time they reached the penthouse, all were Omegas. In fact, they saw no normal humans on the upper floors at all. They entered the penthouse, and there he was ... Hades. There was no mistaking him either; the aura was Beelzebub, Prince of Demons. His hideous, double-headed and winged dragon aura filled the area behind the large desk all the way to the ceiling. The human host was unimpressive, however. A smallish, lean man sat at the desk looking at some documents, while the demon heads swept the room in constant vigilance.

The Assembly's visual perspective stopped suddenly just inside the room when the demon, ram-horned heads stopped their roaming and focused directly on them. Even in the glow of the bright red aura, the four red eyes blazed toward them. The Assembly's visual invasion was invisible, but the demon heads obviously sensed them somehow. The Assembly remained still and back at Mount Olympus those of the Assembly were all actually holding their breath, fearing that the demon aura would hear them.

The man at the desk looked up at them and his face broke into a sinister smile. Hades spoke, his voice dripping with sarcasm, "Hello, Zeus, my brother. It's been a very long time, and it's so very nice of you to visit me. I've been expecting you, but I had hoped you would show up in person. You have caused me much trouble, and you need to die."

225

Zeus felt the invisible fingers of power slowly slipping around them, a power he had not felt in thousands of years, a power he himself had used to defeat his father, Cronus. Hades' mistake was talking to much; that had always been his problem. While Hades delayed, talking, Zeus sped them out of there before the fingers could close. They heard Hades bellow his rage at his mistake.

Zeus said, "Well, Assembly, that was close, but now we know that Hades does have powers. If he would have completed his grip on our personas he could have followed us back to Mount Olympus. If he found out where we are he might have been able to launch attacks on us. But, he failed, and we learned that he does have powers. Seve, to answer your original questions ... no we can't teleport a bomb there, in fact we would be unable to teleport into his area of power at all."

Hera/Augie interrupted, "We still need to go after him, at least go after those Omegas in the building."

Zeus said, "No! We cannot enter the Rose building. That is what Hades hopes we will do. I would wager that the entire building is wired to blow or, more likely, plumbed for gas, and I don't mean for cooking. That has to be his exodus plan for his Omegas, but he is waiting for some of us to enter so he can take some of us out, too. I also suspect that he already has an exodus plan in place for himself that doesn't involve killing his host body. That would set him back to start over in a new body. I will notify Poseidon of our concerns and let him work out a human plan and solution."

# Chapter 15
# The War Continues

As they watched in the mist they were surprised to see an army of vigilantes begin to storm Congress before the deployed military army could arrive. Unfortunately, DC police and security forces, mostly all Omega, had placed forces around the complex and began shooting into the vigilantes. The attacking vigilantes were after the Omegas in congress and mostly armed only with swords and machetes and weren't expecting a gun battle. Many fell before they retreated.

Athena screamed out, "We can't let these people die for us. We need to attack the Omegas."

Zeus bellowed out, "No! That's what Hades wants us to do. He has plans to kill us in some way. You will die if you enter the capital building."

Athena said, "We just can't stop fighting just because we might get killed. We could have been killed many times over, and we are still alive."

Silence fill the chamber as they all considered what was said. Silence stretched over many long minutes, but it was the twins, Jack and Jill (Apollo and Artemis), that broke the silence and said in unison, "We can fight them without worry about being killed." Silence again filled the chamber.

Zeus said, "What are you talking about? There is always a danger of being killed when we fight. All they have to do is kill our bodies."

Jack and Jill took turns saying the words that echoed through the chamber. "We can keep our bodies protected here in Mount Olympus and send our auras out to battle. If they can't kill our bodies they can't kill our Alpha auras."

After another long silence where they were all looking around at each other, Augie said, "Is that even possible?"

Jack and Jill continued, "Our Japanese counterparts, well, us, remember when none here believed our auras could battle with us. We didn't know that it was impossible and simply did it. We think this is the same. Zeus, in ancient times we remember seeing you soar through the sky as a giant eagle launching lightning bolts from your talons."

"This is true." Zeus said, "But conditions were much different back then. Then we were mostly energy and we could change shapes at will; now we are mostly physical in body."

Augie felt the thoughts as Hera began to mouth the words. Luckily she was able to influence Hera's outburst before she could blast Zeus for taking human form so he could fornicate with human women. It might have ended the discussion before it could really begin, and she, like all the others, judging from their absolute attentiveness, was deeply interested in the direction of this discussion.

Hermes/Seve was the first to respond saying, "Yes, I think it is possible. It's true we are subject to physical rules governing the human bodies, but we must not forget about the Alpha power conveyed to the bodies we occupy ... share. The auras themselves proves this fact, and my young friend and partner, Seve does not limited his thinking. He believes we can do anything we allow ourselves to believe possible, and I think he is right. We just have to make it happen."

Zeus said with some authority, "Very well. Twins, It was your idea. Go make it happen."

Seve knew that the key to separating the aura from the human host must happen through the power of the dais, which was controlled by the powers inherent to the Alpha spirit. From his experience with the dais he knew that virtually anything was possible through the dais if you believed it possible. He didn't know how it worked, but it worked. Hermes had worked through the dais all of his existence, but Seve doubted that even Hermes understood it. Seve was determined to make it work and took the lead in directing the other warriors by example. The others watched as he and Hermes sat at their individual dais. He thought he knew how it would work, and if correct, it should be simple. It would require each warrior to maintain constant control of their aura through their own individual dais. This turned out to be the biggest problem.

Heracles and the other original warriors had little accessible operational memories or recent experience with the dais, so he had to take them through the whole process of expanding their dais in their quarters and operating it. This turned out to be the most time consuming and difficult part of the process, but once this was completed he showed them how to send their auras off through the mist as an extenuation of their minds. It was as if all the senses and perspectives of the body projected off with the auras, while their bodies remained safe and somewhat dormant at the dais in their quarters in Mount Olympus.

Seve and Hermes successfully made the transition and transported their antlered deer aura to just outside the capital building and into the midst of the demon police and security force. As the others watched in the mist, their aura, them, was immediately attacked. Swords and bullets passed right through them without harm as they had hoped. Unfortunately, the deer aura could do little damage, but they quickly developed a plan and burst off at a fast pace, immediately followed by a screeching and screaming herd of red demons.

At the first sight of their gleaming, golden aura the demons lost all control and came for them en mass. Initially he really had no plan, actually he was more surprised to find out that the transition had worked. All they could come up with was running, since that is what deer do, but a plan quickly developed. They led the demon horde toward where the vigilantes had retreated, and as they turned around a corner they found them gathered. The vigilantes saw their golden aura chased by the demons and immediately spread out to allow the totally focused and berserk horde ignore and pass between them. Then the vigilantes fell upon the demons from all sides devastating them. It was over quickly.

Heracles bellowed, "Get me down there! I need to fight."

Augie, standing behind the gathered warriors said, "Get yourself down there. That's how it works."

There was no way Heracles was going to miss out on a battle and chance to kill Omega demons and bolted out, headed for his quarters to project his aura. He was quickly followed by the other warriors.

Augie quickly returned to the main dais to report the success of the warriors, and soon the gods were watching the scene outside the capital building. Heracles' aura was soon seen materializing on the steps of the capital building. Amazingly, his raging bull aura had expanded and was complete with thick, pawing legs and even steam escaping from his nostrils. Heracles remained rational enough to wait for the others before entering the capital, but that didn't take long. Athena's giant owl aura was next, followed by Asteria's panther, Eli's dragon, Apollo and Artemis' gorillas, and the ever ready Ares' wolverine. Kerrie's weaving snakes appeared next. Then to her surprise she saw Sue's golden Eagle materialize. After the initial shock she realized that Sue was now merged with Aphrodite and no longer a little girl alone.

For once they had the definite advantage. Now they could safely wage war against Omega without fear. With this discovery they knew they would win the war, and it was only a matter of time. The more she thought about it the more jealous she became. She wanted to join her friends in this battle. Suddenly she realized that each aura was controlled by each individual, and there was no requirement or necessity for the main dais's support. With this realization she said, "We are not needed here, and I think I want to join them in this battle."

Zeus' face uncharacteristically cracked open with a big smile and astonished everyone at the

231

assembly when he said, "You are correct, and I believe I will join you."

They both remained at the main dais and after only a few minutes of experimenting sent their auras traveling through space.

The remaining gods watched the golden lion and bear auras materialize among the other warriors. There were no demons remaining outside, so all the warriors charged the main entrance. As they entered Karrie's snakes began their magical, rhythmic weaving slowing time. With time slowed any action Hades might evoke to release the Omega souls would take too long to save them ... hopefully.

In force the Alpha warriors stormed the capital building immediately attacking the surprised Congressmen and Senators. Due to the crisis situation both Congress and Senate Omegas were gathered together. All the fish were in one pond and easy picking. Time was slowed and the warriors began killing at will, working their way through the building, and by this time the vigilantes had blocked all other exits from the building.

The battle was pure slaughter as the Alpha warriors ravished the demons, and without bodies to hold them back, Athena's giant owl and little Sue's great eagle rose in flight above the demons swooping down with claws to maul the demons and easily slicing off heads with the sweep of their wings. All the warriors were working their way through the hundreds of demons wreaking havoc, but the two new additions of a golden lion and bear bounding side by side through the demons ripping with huge claws and fangs and biting, ripping off and slinging heads was awesome to witness and frightful to see if you were a demon. Many demons in fear tried to exit the building and slaughter inside, only to run into vigilantes attacking and killing them or pushing them back into the building. The inside of the capital building was being painted with blood. Lifeless bodies and heads with sightless eyes adorned the building stared at nothing.

As was his usual position, Heracles' aura led the team and had advances well ahead and somewhat separated from the group. About half of the Omegas had already been killed when the invisible poison gas was released within the building. Heracles noticed the Omega human hosts falling to the floor ahead of him. He continued destroying them before the human bodies completely failed. Many of the devilish auras were withering and dying, but he could see other auras begin to float free. It was too late to destroy these Omega spirit. Hades had been successful in saving many.

As he stood there watching the escaping Omega spirits he noticed that they didn't float away like usual; instead they began to float toward him. As they closed upon him the auras mutated into long bands of binding and began to wrap around him, tightening. He slashed at them with his horns, but they had no substance. The web began tightening and restricting his movements, and a flash of fear swept over him. He tried to run, but he could not move. Through a thickening haze of red he saw the other warriors come and began trying to pull the bands away, but nothing seemed to work. He was completely subdued, and the pressure was becoming painful. The pain became unbearable and mercifully blackness took over.

Zeus saw what was happening to Heracles too late. Then he saw the bands heading for other warriors. Zeus immediately returned to his body and telepathically ordered the other warriors to immediately return before they too could be captured.

***

Mojo knew it was just a matter of time before the Alphas came after his Omegas in the capital building, and he was waiting for them. It was just too big of a temptation. If they came within the building they would die. Mojo already had the gas installed to kill all the host human bodies but waited for the Alphas. If he was lucky he would be able to kill the hosts of the Alphas as well, and he had a plan to kill them once and for all.

He didn't have the power of telepathy as Zeus and the Olympian gods had, but he had a vast deployment of Earth technology. He had direct communication with the Senate Majority Leader and Speaker of the House and several others, who relayed his instructions to the other Omegas, and he could monitor the activities through the camera system. All the unpossessed, those he did not control, had been vacated from the capital building, so Zeus' attack was imminent.

When the attack came it was sudden, and the cursed Alphas slowed time. Although expected, he had not anticipated the number of Alphas to attack and the reduction of time. He also had not expected the attack to consist only of the auras. He didn't have time to analyze the situation, only to react. He ordered the gas to be released immediately; however, it was far too slow, and he lost far more Omegas than he intended.

By them attacking with only the auras he lost the opportunity to kill the Alpha human host, but this didn't alter his plan. He had hoped to kill all the human hosts and free the spirits so his freed Omegas could attack the Alpha spirits. If his plan was successful there would be a far superior number of Omega spirits all ordered to leech on to the Alpha spirits and drain them of their life.

Unfortunately, due to the slowing of time, increased number of Alphas, and speed of the attack, far too many Omega spirits were killed before their hosts could be gassed to release their spirits. His rage boiled within him as he watched his plan being foiled.

It wasn't a total loss however; one of the Alpha's aura, he wasn't sure which one, had ventured farther from the others. When he commanded the Senate Majority Leader to release the gas, he also ordered the Omegas to concentrate on that one in front. He then monitored and watched as the released Omega spirits attacked the aura.

As previously instructed, the Omega spirits transformed into a band and stretch out toward the lone Alpha. As the bands came into contact, they wrapped around it. There were enough Omega spirits to completely encapsulate the aura within a red cocoon of energy. Mojo smiled at its futile efforts to escape, and before the cocoon solidified he could see the pain. They would suck its energy and eventually kill the Alpha, and once that was done, the human host would also die, but he didn't care about the human host. It was useless. He had found a way to kill the Alphas, and they would all soon die in this painful death.

***

Karrie was the first one to reach the chamber. She was visibly upset and screaming, "We can't leave Heracles down their! We have to go get him."

The other warriors had also found their way into the chamber, and all were looking at him for answers, but he really didn't have any answers, because he had no idea what Hades had done. This was something completely new. He began thinking out loud, "We had to get out of there before more of the demons could attach to our auras and capture or kill us as well. I don't think they can kill him unless they have his body, and we can't teleport Heracles's aura back to Mount Olympus until we are able to remove the demons. Heracles himself must teleport his aura. Even if we could, we would be bringing the demons back with him, and I don't know what harm they could do if they gained access to Mount Olympus. We can't take a chance of that.

Karrie countered, "I saw his limp body at his dais, and I couldn't wake him. He is still within his aura and can't get back. I think they might be able to kill his body eventually if they can keep him captured. We have to do something."

Zeus asked, "We have never separated the aura from the body before. Do any of you have any suggestions?" After a few moments of silence Zeus said, "Hermes, do you know what has happened and how the demon auras have survived?

236

Hermes remained in deep concentration for a while then said, "I am not sure just what transformation has taken place in the aura, but auras can't survive for long without a human host. So, if they have already merged within another human host, and I don't believe that's the case without a dais, that they could separate from their human host. This ability is exclusive to the Alpha spirit and the dais. Therefore, in this form their time would be limited, maybe a day at most."

"So, if they can't hope to keep Heracles captured, Hades must intend to kill Heracles," Augie said. How would he do that if his body is here?"

Zeus said, "Thanks to Mr. Henderson's vast knowledge of Earth's technology I think I might know Hades' intent. He is intending to drain Heracles' aura energy. The demon auras are leaching and feeding on the energy from Heracles' aura, and once that is complete the aura and the host body will die. If they are feeding on the Alpha aura they may be able to survive for a longer period of time, long enough to kill Heracles."

Karrie bellowed, "I will not allow that to happen. I will go to him and join with him inside his demon prison. He can feed on my energy and we will fight our way out together."

Zeus said, "You can't do that. You would also be captured. You will both die. I can't allow that."

Indignant, Karrie said, "I'm going, and you can't stop me!" She promptly stood and marched off to her quarters and dais, leaving the others to stare. The others knew there was no stopping her and didn't try.

Karrie/Helen rushed to her own dais determined to help Heracles. She didn't want to live without him anyway. She also realized that her deep love for Heracles was from ancient lives and not from her own experiences as Karrie. Still, the love she felt for Heracles was real, and she would not lose him if there was anything she could do. If she died in the process ... well so be it.

As her aura merged with Heracles she felt the resistance of the demons, but the red bindings were positioned to keep Heracles' aura inside and not to prevent hers from entering. As she entered she felt the immense pressure and pain that Heracles was enduring. He was weak and felt his energy being sucked from him by the demons, and she felt her energy flow into Heracles, and she calculated that her energy would not last long at the rate it was being drained. She had to slow the rate and slowed time. As she stopped time the drain was immediately reduced, gaining her time to evaluate Heracles' condition.

He was weak from the struggle and felt injured, and that was something she could correct. She called upon her healing powers and began to reach out for the healing energy. Her shock was immediate when she was flooded with this healing energy. Suddenly she understood why. Her healing energy was coming from the demon aura binding. Now instead of the demons draining her energy she was pulling theirs. The drain was still there, but her healing blue energy was more than replenishing Heracles' and her auras. In fact she was able to begin healing Heracles, and soon he was awake and aware of her presence and their strengthening auras' power.

As she continued to drain the demons' power she felt the binding begin to weaken, and the red glow was becoming almost transparent. She increased her concentration and seized hard on the healing energy, and suddenly there was a loud pop as the bindings vanished in a puff of red smoke.

They didn't take time to congratulate each other on their victory, and immediately transported back to their bodies at Mount Olympus.

***

Mojo continued to watch the tightening cocoon squeezing the life out of the Alpha enclosed and enjoyed it immensely, but something abruptly changed. One moment the Alpha was still and lifeless and the next the cocoon began to shake and rock, like a hatching egg. Then he noticed a slight bluish glow within the cocoon that slowly grew in brilliance until bright rays of the blue light escaped the cocoon shooting in all directions. The brilliant rays grew in thickness until the cocoon busts open with a loud pop. His Omega spirits seemed to burn into red smoke and dissolve into nothingness. Emerging from the smoke stood the golden bull aura, angry and searching for a target, but there were none.

Floating beside the bull aura were two giant, blue glowing snakes weaving back and forth, also searching. After a moment both auras snapped out of existence. The damned Alphas had escaped back to Mount Olympus.

He hadn't seen the second aura arrive, but obviously it teleported inside the cocoon after it was formed, and he recognized the source of the blue glow. It came from the healing power of an Alpha. He hadn't seen that glow for thousands of years and thought that power no longer existed. Apparently one of the awaking surviving Alphas possessed this power ... damn Zeus and his interference.

The one good thing that came from this engagement was the fact that Zeus would now have fear for his Alpha aura attacks, since he had almost lost one of his precious Alphas and would have had it not been for the healer.

Still, for him it was time to get his Omegas out of America and consider this land lost to him. He had the rest of the world, however, and it was time to consolidate his power and control over it. Most of his important Omegas had been lost here, and once the remaining ones were out, he might as well totally destroy this country.

Mojo issued the evacuation orders. He didn't dare use ground transportation, because they would be spotted and killed by the Alpha warriors, military or the damn vigilantes roaming the country. He had lost large numbers of Omegas, but he still had a large number of Omegas hiding that he needed to evacuate. He had already booked all the cruise ships, those he didn't already own, on the East and West coast and helicopters were standing by to transport his warriors to the cruise ships. Of course, the ships were also prepared to release the Omega spirits if necessary. Once the ships were loaded and at sea he would have total control over them.

His personal jet, that made Air Force One look like a Piper Cub in comparison, was standing by at his private airport to take him directly to Iran and his new headquarters in Tehran. Iran was chosen because Russia would be his instrument of destruction for America and could wind up a radioactive waste heap from retaliation from America. He had also begun the evacuation from his headquarters in Moscow, but many of those in control would be required to launch the attack. They had also been ordered to kill their hosts and free their Omega spirit before America retaliated.

***

When Karrie/Helen and Heracles, hand in hand, returned to the main Assembly they were greeted with cheers, uncharacteristic for the gods. Karrie was bombarded with questions that she tried to answer as best she could. She unquestionably had been foolish to join with Heracles, but lucky to discover the extent of her powers and lucky that her healing power had been able to draw energy from Omega auras. In healing Heracles she had discovered how the healing power provided an effective defense against the demons' attack.

Zeus confirmed her thoughts when he said, "Hades' changed the rules by the nature of his attack, just like we did by sending our auras to fight. By doing what we did we might have won the war, but unfortunately, he took that sure victory away. I'm positive that he didn't anticipate our ability to send our aura into battle, and had you gone in human form he just might have been able to kill your human body by what he did. His attack didn't destroy us as he had hopped, but he now knows that he has found a method to neutralize our new form of attack. Had Helen's counterattack not worked he might have won the war. We were lucky."

241

"In the future when we battle we must limit our exposure and be prepared to immediately evacuate if we can't kill the Omega spirits outright. Once Hades kills the Omega hosts and releases the spirits we must assume they will attack us, and there is only one healer, Helen. If they attack more than one at a time we might be in trouble. She must be protected."

Helen was a little embarrassed at all the attention. Everyone was staring at her, and that is when she noticed Sean and the cameras pointed at her. Helen looked directly at Sean and said, "Was all this broadcast to the world? Now I'm really embarrassed."

Sean smiled and said, "Not all. We cut some of the discussion and planning, but the battle in Congress for sure and your battle with the cocoon ... absolutely. You can bet you have more fan clubs now."

***

It had been days since they heard from Admiral Neece and Jack Ward and contacted them to suggested they bring them back to Mount Olympus for a conference. Admiral Neece and Jack Ward readily agreed and soon began to shimmer and materialize in the mist. They quickly assumed their ancient positions on their thrones.

Zeus had immediately warned both gods of Hades' change of attack strategy so they wouldn't be caught off guard, but now he caught them up on their ability to send their aura to do battle, which they seemed extremely interested in but showed no real surprise. Zeus described the last battle in which they almost lost Heracles and Helen and how

242

Helen's healing powers had destroyed the demon auras and saved Heracles.

Poseidon actually laughed and said, "Brother, you forget that Sean and his crew are still transmitting to the world, and the whole world, well except those areas blacked out, watched the 'Battle for the Capital', as they are calling it. I also watched the battle on TV." As Poseidon spoke Jack Ward began emphatically nodding, confirming that many have been following the activities of the Olympians and that he had also watched the battle on TV.

Zeus had to admit to himself that Sean and the New York Times reporter had become fixtures at Mount Olympus, and he and the others hardly noticed them. But, if the world was watching, then so was Hades, and he began racking his brain to remember just what secrets may have been transmitted to him by oversight. He was unaccustomed to the world watching their activities, but he saw no serious reason to stop it now. He did, however, say, "Sean, I must rely on you to (What's the word you people use?) 'Censor' your broadcasts, so we don't give away any secrets to the enemy. Okay?"

Sean said, "Yes, sir. We have done that a few times already."

"Very well." Zeus said to Sean, then continued speaking to Poseidon and Jack, "I guess you don't need a report from us, so I guess you can continue with your briefing."

Admiral Neece began, "There is quite a lot to report, actually. After the 'Battle for the Capital' the enthusiastic vigilantes launched a massive drive across the nation. I can report that together we have taken back our country. What Omegas that remained evacuated or are in the process of evacuating. They are on cruise ships headed for points east. We don't know where yet. All government agencies have been cleared, the President is back in the White House, and the valid Congress is back at work trying to clean up the disaster the Omegas created. It will take a long time to clean up, but with the Omegas out of the picture it will happen."

"Jack tells me that the FBI has created a DNA data base to catalog the Titan descendants of both Alpha and Omega. It will take a while to gather all the data, but it's coming. The Omega descendants will be flagged and on a watch list for the future."

"Now, Sean, this is one of those times we need to stop transmission." After the equipment was turned off, Admiral Neece continued. "The war between Alphas and Omegas will never end until one side has wiped out the other. I hope the winner will be us. Earth is doomed if we don't win, but as we seem to be winning at the moment, the Earth might still be doomed. I say this because we have to wonder what Hades is thinking and planning.

Since Hades is evacuating America we have to wonder what he has in mind. He knows he lost America, but the entire world is his domain. To the rest of the world he can't appear to be losing. The top thinkers and planners of the American military, and I agree with them, believe he will try to destroy America. Since he has lost using Omega warriors to destroy American from within, we believe he will try to destroy us using a human method from outside. By that I mean human war, and the easiest way is nuclear. I believe it's inevitable."

"The deterrent against a nuclear war has always been the fear of mutual destruction, but Hades will not care about that as long as he survives along with most of his Omegas. For this reason we believe he and his escaping Omegas will settle in the Mid-East, probably in Tehran, Iran, and force Russia to attack us. Hades still has much control in Russia. If he does launch a nuclear attack, America will not survive. There is no way the military could possibly prevent all the missiles from striking here. Of course Russia would not survive either, but Hades wouldn't care, and he could rebuild."

"Many Titans might argue that this is not our concern, because it would be a human war, and we should not get involved. They would say Mount Olympus would survive, and our responsibility is to our own war with the Omegas. I would argue that Hades is the cause, and we must help the humans survive." After this last statement he fell silent and waited for a response.

Poseidon didn't have to wait long as Zeus immediately took up the gauntlet saying, "A few weeks ago I might have been one of those arguing against helping the humans, but now I'm almost as much human as I am Titan, thanks to Mr. Henderson. Not only that, but we wouldn't have survived this far without the help of humans. Thanks to them Hades has had to evacuate America, and if we win this war it will be because of help from other humans. So, to answer your unasked question, yes, we will do everything we can do to save them. Are we all in agreement?" Unanimous nods met his stare around the assembly.

"I am, however, afraid the Assembly on Titan would make that very argument, and we can expect no help from them. So what help to Earth must come from us, and I'm not sure just what that could be. We are stronger now that we are merged with humans, still I'm not sure if we are not strong enough alone to evoke a shield in space to protect against a missile attack. We will have to consider all the options available to us."

"Sean, as you see, the people of Earth shouldn't know about this. It would cause mass panic, and Hades might know our plans."

Sean said, "Yes, of course I understand, but the people of Earth should know that the Olympians are fighting for them as well. If we survive I would like to tell them."

"Very well."

***

Forty-eight hours later Admiral Neece was notified in his office, now at the Pentagon, of the missile launches in Russia and immediately telepathically told Zeus. They hadn't yet discussed any planned defense options, so he was somewhat surprised when Zeus responded with instructions.

Zeus said, "We will also launch our defenses from Mount Olympus. Watch Fox News Network, and you will know if we are successful. Use all your defenses, but wait on any retaliatory missile launches unless we are unsuccessful. I don't want you to destroy any more humans than necessary, even Russian. Maybe Russia can be saved, but if we fail do what you must. And, also take out

Hades' headquarters in Tehran. Nuke them out! Make the Omegas start over, and give the free humans a chance to revolt."

Luckily, the president hadn't revoked Martial Law and he still had control. Admiral Neece notified the president of his actions and gave all the necessary instructions to comply with Zeus' directions, then tuned in to Fox to watch.

As Poseidon watched his monitor in amazement, a team of Alpha auras appeared in the Mount Olympus' mist. From the view they blinked into existence high above the Earth. He immediately recognized Zeus leading the group of warriors. The golden lion was hard to miss, but the addition of large, widespread wings came as a surprise. The wings pulled against nonexistent air and propelled him through space at a staggering pace. Close behind him was the unmistakable huge golden owl of Athena, but what caught his attention was the shimmering lightning bolts carried in the claws of the owl.

Athena had always been the favorite of Zeus, and he had been known to allow Athena to use the power of his lightning bolts in ancient times. Poseidon knew immediately what Zeus had in mind and cheered. He had no idea how Zeus had made this all work, but obviously he had.

The others in the team of Alpha warriors were both surprising and not so surprising. All those with wings were present: Sue/Aphrodite's golden eagle raced alongside Athena, Col. Blevins/Demeter's golden winged horse, Pegasus, followed beside Eli's winged golden dragon. The most surprising was the auras of Apollo and

Artemis (Jack & Jill) as they rode Pegasus and the dragon. Apollo and Artemis' golden gorillas held mighty bows, for which they were famous, with a quiver of golden arrows strapped to their back.

The warriors folded their wings and dove toward the rising ballistic missiles emerging from the atmosphere into space. There were many, and they were illuminated as if by magic, or more likely Olympian powers, and easily identified. Zeus began launching powerful and shimmering bolts of lightning streaking across space to engulf missile after missile causing them to blossom in intense white light and instantly explode into a dazzling fiery display. Athena and Aphrodite joined the assault launching lightning bolts of their own. Apollo and Artemis shot golden arrows, that were far more than arrows. The blazing arrows darted across space to encompass the rising missiles in golden flame. The warriors darted in every direction and at great distances, never missing. The atmosphere filled with flaming meteorites burning up as they fell back to Earth. Those missiles that curved into space for their supersonic trajectory toward America were soon caught by the warriors and dealt with a fiery death. Only a few missiles even approach America, and none made it.

Admiral Neece, the Olympians and the world watched in awe as the battle in space took place. Even he had a hard time believing it. Zeus and the warriors had done well. They had saved America, and he was proud of them.

Zeus had thought long and hard about Admiral Neece's prediction of a nuclear attack and quickly realized that the battle would be in space and very

248

quick. The missiles' trajectory would be in space above the atmosphere and at supersonic speed, and any defense would have to match those requirements.

The actual power to be used to destroy missiles was never in question. His lightning bolts traveled at the speed of light and over great distances instantly. His trusted daughters Athena and Aphrodite were the only others that he had trained and trusted with the power. The only other power and weapon that could work over great distances would be the magical golden arrows of the twins, Apollo and Artemis. This ability narrowed the choices of warriors to him and these warriors.

Breathing in space would also not be a problem for the auras, but the ability to fly without air and at supersonic speeds was a problem. The power of the dais allowed teleportation, but altering the location would be the problem. Then the solution came to him. By merging the mental process required to fly using wings with the thoughts required for teleportation they could achieve a constantly changing teleportation location, even the simulation of flight. Yes, this would work, but only two of these warriors had wings. He was not worried about himself, since he had once existed as pure energy and remembered how to build and alter a physical body. Many times in those previous bodies he had had wings. He liked his current aura, but it would not be difficult to add wings to his golden lion. Unfortunately, however, his children had never existed in pure energy form and wouldn't know how. Oh, they might figure it out, but it would require a human's lifetime to develop. Okay, who had wings? He then smiled, because he now had the full solution. He called his team.

As soon as Zeus and the warriors returned to Mount Olympus after the battle, they were met with cheers from all present, and Sean Brannon was the loudest of all. The celebration was part of Sean's renewed television transmission and commentary, and he led off with, "Ladies and gentlemen, fellow Americans, and world viewers, if there was ever any doubt that the Alphas are our friends and on our side, this last battle in space should remove any doubt. This was a human war and attack, and the Alphas just saved us from nuclear destruction. This was not part of the alien war, and by all rights they could have stayed out of it and concentrated on their own war. But, the Alphas have proved they are our friends and heroes of Earth, and we should also do anything we can to help them, because helping them is helping ourselves. Together we have taken back America and with our help our neighbors Canada and Mexico will soon follow, but still much of the world remains under Omega control.

Their war is far from over, but I think, together, we are ready for the next step.

# THE END